CW00959143

CELEBRATION AFTER DARK

GANSETT ISLAND SERIES, BOOK 14

MARIE FORCE

Celebration After Dark
Gansett Island Series, Book 14
By: Marie Force

Published by HTJB, Inc.
Copyright 2015. HTJB, Inc.
Cover design by Courtney Lopes
Interior Layout by Isabel Sullivan, E-book Formatting Fairies

ISBN: 978-1942295402

If you're reading this book and did not purchase it, or it was not purchased for your use only, then please return it and purchase your own copy. Thank you for respecting the hard work of this author. To obtain permission to excerpt portions of the text, please contact the author at marie@marieforce.com.

All characters in this book are fiction and figments of the author's imagination.

www.marieforce.com

For the Gansett Island fans who've embraced the McCarthy family from the beginning—this one's for you.

McCarthys of Gansett Island

Family Tree

Mallory Vaughn
(DAUGHTER OF "BIG MAC" MCCARTHY
AND DIANA VAUGHN (DECEASED))

"Big Mac" McCarthy MARRIED TO Linda McCarthy

Mac McCarthy Jr.
MARRIED TO
Maddie Chester McCarthy

Grant McCarthy
MARRIED TO
Stephanie Logan McCarthy

Adam McCarthy
ENGAGED TO
Abby Callahan

Evan McCarthy
ENGAGED TO
Grace Ryan

Janey McCarthy Cantrell
MARRIED TO
Joe Cantrell

Thomas and Hailey
(CHILDREN OF MAC & MADDIE)

Charlie Grandchamp
(STEPFATHER TO STEPHANIE)
ENGAGED TO
Sarah Lawry

P.J. Cantrell
(SON OF JANEY & JOE)

Francine Chester Saunders MARRIED TO Ned Saunders

Seamus O'Grady MARRIED TO Carolina O'Grady (MOTHER TO JOE)

Tiffany Chester Taylor (DAUGHTER OF FRANCINE) MARRIED TO Blaine Taylor

Ashleigh Sturgil
DAUGHTER OF TIFFANY TAYLOR
AND JIM STURGIL

(BROTHER TO "BIG MAC")

Judge Frank McCarthy, WAS MARRIED TO Joann McCarthy (DECEASED)
IS DATING Betsy Jacobson

Dr. Kevin McCarthy IS DIVORCED FROM Deb McCarthy

Riley McCarthy
SON OF KEVIN AND DEB

Finn McCarthy
SON OF KEVIN AND DEB

Laura McCarthy Lawry
(DAUGHTER OF FRANK AND JOANN) MARRIED TO
Owen Lawry

Shane McCarthy
(SON OF FRANK AND JOANN) ENGAGED TO
Katie Lawry

Holden Newsome
SON OF LAURA MCCARTHY LAWRY
AND JUSTIN NEWSOME

Sarah Lawry (MOTHER OF OWEN SEPARATED FROM Mark Lawry
ENGAGED TO
Charlie Grandchamp

Adele MARRIED TO Russ Kincaid (DAUGHTER OF SARAH LAWRY, GRANDPARENTS TO LAWRY SIBLINGS)

Owen Lawry
MARRIED TO
Laura McCarthy Lawry

Julia Lawry

Katie Lawry
ENGAGED TO
Shane McCarthy

Josh Lawry

Cindy Lawry

John Lawry

Jeff Lawry

McCarthy Family Friends

Luke Harris
MARRIED TO
Sydney Donovan Harris

Dan Torrington
ENGAGED TO
Kara Ballard

David Lawrence
AND
Daisy Babson

Jenny Wilks
MARRIED TO
Alex Martinez

Jared James
MARRIED TO
Elizabeth "Lizzie" Sutter

Marion Martinez
(MOTHER TO ALEX AND PAUL MARTINEZ)

Paul Martinez
(SON OF GEORGE (DECEASED) AND MARION,
BROTHER TO ALEX)
ENGAGED TO
Hope Russell

CHAPTER 1

Mac McCarthy Senior, known to all as Big Mac, woke on the morning of December twentieth to the distinctive sounds of winter on Gansett Island—howling wind, icy snow pinging against the windows and groaning beams in the house he'd called home for nearly four decades. But today was not any average winter day. On this day forty years ago, he married the love of his life. Today was a day for celebration.

The kids were throwing a party later that Mac and Linda weren't supposed to know about. "Voodoo Mama," as the kids called Linda, knew everything they were up to. She'd picked up on the scent of a party months ago, which was why they hadn't planned one for themselves. He had a few surprises of his own to mark the occasion that he couldn't wait to give her.

She slept curled up to him, the way she did every night. Even on the few occasions when they'd been at odds, she always reached for him in her sleep. Their marriage had been filled with love and joy and five incredible kids who'd been the light of their lives. Each of them had found their soul mate in the last few years, which was the only thing he and Linda had ever truly wanted for them.

Nothing made Big Mac more content than seeing his kids happy and in love with people he would've hand-chosen for each of them. Mac with Maddie, Grant with Stephanie, Adam with Abby, Evan with Grace and Janey with Joe. All of them perfect matches in every way that mattered.

In addition to his own five, he'd been like a father to Luke Harris, the young man who'd worked for him at the marina since he was fourteen, and who was now happily married to his first love, Sydney Donovan Harris, with a baby on the way.

A few years ago, Big Mac had made Mac and Luke his partners in the marina, which was one of the best things he'd ever done. It freed him up to relax a little while the two young guys put their considerable energy into steering the business into the modern era. Big Mac was more than happy to take a backseat to them. He had grandchildren to coddle, bullshit to shoot, fish to catch and a wife to take traveling as he'd promised her he would once the kids were launched and the businesses were in good hands.

And then there was Mallory Vaughn, the woman who'd appeared earlier in the year with the life-changing news that she was the daughter he'd never known he had, the product of a brief relationship that ended before he met Linda. Talk about shocking! But Linda had set the tone, accepting Mallory into their family and making sure her arrival didn't turn into a crisis for them. He'd never loved his gorgeous wife more than he had watching her welcome his daughter into their home and family.

The bedside clock read 6:20, which was far too early to wake Linda to begin the celebration. With nowhere to be for hours, they had the day to themselves before the party. That was plenty of time to shower her with the gifts he'd spent months organizing, among other things he wanted to do today.

He was kind of glad it was snowing. The men of the family had been spending every possible minute helping his son Mac and nephew Shane with the addition to the home of their friends Seamus and Carolina O'Grady, who'd recently taken in two young boys after their mother's tragic death. Everyone wanted to see the new family settled as soon as possible, and they were down to finish work on the addition. With the storm raging outside, Big Mac could justify a day off to spend with his wife.

In the meantime, he found his thoughts wandering back in time to the summer day when he first laid eyes on the woman who would become the center of his life. He'd been home in Providence to close on the ramshackle marina that several people had told him not to buy. His dad had been particularly vociferous in his objections.

"Your grandmother left you that money so you could make something of yourself, Mac," his father had said. "She'd be very disappointed to see you pissing it away on a hunk of junk in the middle of nowhere."

"I'm sorry you think so, Dad, but I've got a feeling about this place. With a little love and a lot of work, I think I can turn it into a gold mine."

"And how do you plan to *eat* while you're waiting to strike gold?"

"I've got my charter captain's license and feelers out all over the place. I'll find work. Don't worry." As long as he was near the water in some way or another, Mac was confident he could make a living somehow.

Frank McCarthy Senior shook his head with disgust and dismay over the plans his middle son had made for his little corner of Gansett Island.

"Let him be, Frank," Mac's mother, Jane, had said. "He's got to make his own way the same way you made yours. Harping on him isn't going to change his mind, especially when he's signing the papers tomorrow."

Despite his mother's support, Mac had left his parents' home that day feeling dejected and scared for the first time since he'd fallen in love with the marina. What if his dad was right? What if he pissed away the nest egg his grandmother had left him on something that would never pay off?

As he drove the truck he'd bought in high school that was now on its last legs to his brother Frank's place, he blasted Bruce Springsteen's new album *Born to Run* in the tape deck. His chest tightened with anxiety and panic. He'd wagered everything he had and then some on the marina, knowing it needed a load of work to make it presentable. He'd never been afraid of hard work and had been looking forward to getting on with it before his dad filled his head with doubts.

Mac found a parking space two blocks from Frank's house, and after he shut off the engine, he sat there for a minute thinking it through from every angle. One of the lawyers Frank had interned with over the summer had been good enough to look over the contracts for the purchase of the marina and declared them sound. Mac had had the place surveyed, and even though it looked a little rough around the edges to the naked eye, it was structurally sound. He had financing in place for the portion not covered by his inheritance and had money built into the loan for renovations.

It would take years to own the place free and clear, but he still had faith that eventually the investment of his time and money would pay off. And if it didn't? Well, he was a young guy with plenty of time to recover and find something else to do with his life.

He got out of the truck and walked to Frank's apartment, which occupied the first floor of a three-story Victorian. Frank was heading to law school at Brown in the fall and lived there with two other guys. The three of them were hosting this afternoon's party in their backyard. Mac was in bad need of some time with his big brother—not to mention a couple of cold ones.

Mac let himself into the apartment with the key Frank had given him so he could crash on the sofa rather than stay at home where his mother would want him home by midnight and then sniff him, looking for telltale signs that he'd been drinking. It was easier to stay with Frank, who expected him to smell like beer because they usually drank it together.

"Mac!" Frank called from the kitchen door. "Get in here and check out these wings that Brett made. They'll set your mouth on fire."

"And doesn't that sound like fun?"

Frank took a closer look at him. "What's with you?"

"Nothing."

Leaving the kitchen and the wings behind, Frank took Mac by the arm and steered him back the way he'd come. They went through the front door to the porch. "I'll ask again—what's with you?"

Mac hesitated, but only for a second, because this was Frankie, his big brother and best friend. If anyone would tell it to him straight, it was Frank. "Am I making a huge mistake buying the marina?"

"*What?*"

"You heard me. Am I pissing away the money Grandma left me on something stupid?"

"Where's this shit coming from?"

"Something Dad said has me thinking. What if it's a total disaster, and I lose my shirt?"

"What if it's a huge success and you make millions? Have you considered that possibility?"

"Not really. I'd be perfectly satisfied to make a decent living from the place. I'm not looking for millions."

"Still, it's not outside the realm of possibility. People are saying Gansett is the next Martha's Vineyard. Sky's the limit, bro, and you're in on the ground floor."

"You still think it's a good idea to buy the place?"

"If I didn't, I would've said so." Frank was the one person from his life in Providence who'd been out to the island to see the marina, because Mac trusted his brother's instincts and wanted his opinion. "You've got your work cut out for you to undo years of neglect, but that's nothing you can't handle."

Frank's assurances helped to calm the wave of panic that had been growing since Mac left their parents' home.

"You're going to sign those papers tomorrow and take the plunge, because if you don't, you'll spend the rest of your life wondering what might've happened if you had."

"That's very true."

"Sometimes you've just got to go for it, Mac, and let the chips fall where they will. Either it'll be a success or it won't, but the only failure here would be in not trying."

"Thanks, Frankie. That's exactly what I needed to hear."

"Dad means well. You know he does, but sometimes he spouts off without thinking. Don't let him fill your mind with doubts. This is what you want, Mac. Go for it."

"I'm going to."

"Good. You've already sacrificed a lot for that marina." Frank reminded him of the brief but promising relationship with Diana Vaughan that had ended because she wasn't interested in life on a remote island.

Mac had missed her in the months since they broke up, but he knew it had been the right thing to end it now rather than later when it would be harder to reconcile their differing life goals. "Yeah, you're right. Too late to turn back now."

"Yes, it is, and it's going to be great. I know it." Frank's gaze shifted to the street, his smile lighting up his face. "Here comes my girl, and she's brought friends. *Cute* friends."

Mac looked toward the street and saw Joann, Frank's girlfriend since high school, coming down the sidewalk with three other girls in tow. Mac immediately zeroed in on one of them. Petite with long blond hair, she had an arresting face and eyes that danced with glee at something one of her friends had said.

Watching her come closer, Mac felt like he'd been sucker-punched.

"Earth to Mac," Frank said, drawing his attention off the blond goddess.

"W-who is that?"

"Huh?"

"The blond with Joann. Who is she?"

"That's her friend Linda from PC," he said, referring to Providence College.

"Introduce me."

"Um, okay…"

Joann came up the stairs and launched herself at Frankie, laying a wet, sloppy kiss on him. "God, this week was endless."

"For me, too, baby."

The two of them had been mad about each other from the moment they met in high school, when Jo's family moved to the city. Frank had come home from the first day of his sophomore year professing he'd met his future wife, and they'd been together ever since.

Keeping an arm around Joann, Frank said, "Ladies, this is my brother, Mac. Mac, meet Josie, Linda and Kathy."

Linda. Her name is Linda. Mac shook hands with all three women and then gave his full attention to the one in the middle, who stood out in the group of gorgeous women like a shining star. He'd never been so bowled over by a girl—or a woman. She was *all* woman, but giggled like a girl with her friends as they made their way inside with Joann leading the way.

"Easy, big fella," Frank said, his hand on Mac's arm.

"How do you think Linda would feel about living on Gansett Island with an up-and-coming marina owner?

Frank tossed his head back and laughed as hard as Mac had ever seen him laugh.

Too bad Mac was serious.

"You don't do anything halfway, do you, Mac?"

"What's the point of doing something halfway?"

"Go easy so you don't scare her off. She'll think you're some sort of ax murderer if you ask her to come live on your remote island five minutes after you meet her."

"Laugh all you want, Frankie, but that girl is going to live with me on my island. Mark my words."

Shaking his head in amusement, Frank said, "Good thing you're going to have a lawyer in the family. You'll need me to defend you when she files charges against you."

Mac laughed at Frank's joke, but he suspected he'd need his brother to be his best man before he'd ever need his legal services.

Big Mac chuckled at the memory of that long-ago day. It had been ages since he'd thought about how his father had nearly talked him out of buying the marina—and what a mistake that would've been. He'd paid off the loan within five years and had gone on to make millions on the place, just as Frankie had predicted. It hadn't happened overnight, but after the island was featured on a TV show on East Coast destinations two years after he bought the marina, nothing was ever the same.

And speaking of never the same…he was never the same after that day at Frank's house. That was the day his life really began, the day he met Linda.

CHAPTER 2

She laughed—a lot. He knew that because he watched her obsessively, waiting for an opportunity to get her alone so he could talk to her. But she was surrounded by people—male and female—and he got tired of waiting. So he went over to her, prepared to ask her to take a walk with him, to talk to him, to give him even one minute of her attention as well as the rest of her life if she wasn't doing anything.

Then he was standing right in front of her, and every thought in his head abandoned him.

"Help you with something?" she asked, looking way up at him. He towered over her. "It's Mac, right?"

He nodded like the mute he'd become in her presence. "Take a walk," he managed to say. "With me."

"Umm…" She glanced nervously at her friends, who waited expectantly to see what she'd say. "Okay."

With that one word, she gave him hope. He offered her his arm, and when she curled her hand into the crook of his elbow, his heart gave a happy little leap. It was imperative, or so he thought, to get her out of there, away from the admiring eyes of every other guy at the party so she wouldn't meet someone she liked better before he had a chance to convince her that she needed him in her life.

What if she already had someone? That thought struck him like an arrow to the chest, sucking the air from his lungs as he walked with her through the gate that led to the sidewalk. So many young women these days were waiting for boyfriends and husbands to come home now that the dreadful war in Vietnam was finally over. He'd been too young and Frankie had been in college, so neither of them had gone, but lots of other guys they knew were counting down the days until they could come home to girls like Linda.

"Do you have a boyfriend?" he asked out of nowhere, cringing the instant the words left his mouth.

Her ringing laugh followed the awkward question. "Who wants to know?"

"Malcolm John McCarthy, known as Mac, wants to know. Do you?"

"Not at the moment."

"Are you waiting for someone to come home from Vietnam?"

"Only my brother."

Mac had never known relief so profound or so pervasive. "How's it possible a girl like you doesn't have twenty boyfriends vying for her attention?"

She smiled up at him, and he lost what was left of his heart. "You're a charmer, Malcolm John McCarthy, known as Mac."

"Never been before. Must be you."

"Must be."

Walking backward in front of her, he said, "What's your last name?"

"Rudolph."

"Tell me the truth, Linda Rudolph—have you ever harbored a secret burning desire to live on an island?"

"An *island*? Can't say I've ever entertained that particular burning desire."

The implication that she'd entertained others had his full attention, and he had to remind himself they were in public, and he wasn't allowed to let his mind go there—at least not yet.

"Why do you ask?"

"Well, so, it's kind of like this... Tomorrow, I'm signing papers that will make me the proud owner of a ramshackle marina on Gansett Island that I plan to turn into a gold mine. I was wondering if you might like to help me do that."

"Didn't I just meet you an hour ago?"

"Uh-huh."

"And you're asking me to come live with you on your island and help you turn your ramshackle marina into a gold mine. Is that right?"

"That's about it, yep."

"Are you always this forward when you meet someone new?"

"Nope. I've never asked a girl to come live with me anywhere, let alone on my island."

"I'm flattered to be the first, but you'll understand my reluctance, being as I'm in school and all that."

"What year?"

"Going into my junior year."

"I won't be able to wait two years to marry you. There's just no way that'll work for me."

"*Mac!* Are you out of your mind? Do you have some sort of condition that makes you delusional?"

"Do you believe in love at first sight?"

"No! That only happens in the movies."

"And on front porches in Providence."

"You... I..." She pursed her lips, seeming to choose her words carefully. "Are you being serious right now?"

"Dead serious. You ever feel something right here?" He pushed his fist into his gut. "And you know? You just *know*?"

"That hasn't happened to me before."

"It's happened to me only one other time."

"Were you in love with her?"

He smiled at the catty tone to her voice. "As much as you can be in love with a dilapidated group of buildings, a sagging dock and a parking lot full of potholes. I took one look at that mess and felt like I'd come home. And I took one look at you, the most beautiful girl I've ever laid eyes on, and felt like I'd found the other half of me."

Her hand came up to her chest, as if she were trying to remember how to breathe. Maybe he had that thought because he was feeling sort of breathless himself.

"How old are you, Mac?"

"Just turned twenty."

"And you expect me to believe you can take one look at me—at age *twenty*—and think you're going to want me forever?"

"Yes, I expect you to believe that. How old are you?"

"Nineteen."

"Where'd you grow up?"

"In Massachusetts, outside of Boston."

"Ahh, a city girl."

"You're from here, right? Doesn't that make you a city boy?"

"Providence is small potatoes next to Boston." It occurred to him that a girl from Boston might find Gansett Island incredibly boring. "You're on summer vacation, right?"

"I am."

"Are you working?"

"I was supposed to be a nanny for a young family, but the dad's job transferred him unexpectedly, so I'm still looking for something. I'm staying with Josie and Kathy for the summer."

"Come to Gansett with me for the day tomorrow. Take a look at what I'm doing there. I want to know what you think of it." At this point, he was running on pure adrenaline fueled by the gut feeling that she was intended for him. How he knew that, he couldn't say. He just knew.

"You're a very intense young man, Mac."

"I've been told that before, but I don't see any point in doing things halfway," he said, borrowing Frank's words from earlier. "Tomorrow, I'm gambling my future on a marina that may or may not pay off. I want you with me when I go there for the first time as the rightful owner. Will you come?"

Her lips moved to the side as she thought about his offer. After a long moment in which Mac died a thousand deaths waiting for her to reply, she said, "I won't stay there overnight."

"I'll bring you back on the last boat tomorrow night. You have my word."

"Okay. I'll go, then."

Mac blew out a deep breath. Two round trips to the island weren't in the budget, but he'd find the money if it meant he got to show her his dream. "Thank you. Will you do one other thing for me?"

"Depends on what it is."

"Don't go out with anyone else."

"You mean between now and tomorrow when I'm going to Gansett Island with you?"

"I mean ever. Don't go out with anyone but me ever again."

She started to laugh, but it died on her lips when she seemed to get that he meant it.

Because he couldn't wait another second to touch her, he raised his hand to her face and laid it flat against her cheek. Then he ran his thumb over her full bottom lip, loving the sound of her breath catching in her throat. "You're so incredibly beautiful, Linda."

"You're a rather handsome devil yourself, but of course you know that."

"As long as you think so, that's all that matters.'"

"Are you always so insistent when it comes to women?"

"I'm never insistent, because I've never cared enough to be. You're different."

"How do you know that?" she asked in a small voice that had his heart doing that leaping thing again.

"Do you believe in fate? In things that are meant to be?"

"I never have before."

He leaned in to replace his thumb with his lips, a soft fleeting caress that only confirmed what he already knew—she was his. "It might be time to start believing."

*

With the hindsight of four decades, Big Mac had to acknowledge that he was damned lucky she hadn't run from him, screaming for the police.

His low chuckle had her stirring next to him.

"What're you laughing about first thing in the morning?" she asked in the husky, sleepy morning voice he adored.

"I'm thinking about the day we met and how lucky I was that you didn't call the police on me with the way I came on so strong with you."

"You are lucky. The thought crossed my mind. You were awfully forward."

"It was the seventies, babe. Forward was in vogue."

"You took it to a whole other level."

Big Mac turned over, put his arm around her and drew her in snug against him, loving how she fit so perfectly in his arms. "Happy anniversary, my love. I'm so glad you didn't call the cops."

"Me, too, and happy anniversary to you as well."

"Forty years," he said with a sigh. "How's that possible?"

"Went by in the blink of an eye."

"You ever wish you'd called the cops on me that day at Frankie's?"

"Not for one second, as you well know."

"Ever wish you'd finished college?"

"Nope. I would've been so distracted thinking about you that I would've flunked out anyway."

"Sometimes I feel bad about talking you into dropping out to come live with me on my island. I thought your folks would never forgive me for that."

"They loved you as much as I did."

"Not at first. They thought you were shackling yourself to a lunatic."

"They never used that word," she said, making him laugh. "They admired your ambition."

"But they wished I'd been ambitious on the mainland rather than out here."

"They understood why we wanted to be here. They loved coming out in the summers to spend a few weeks every year."

"I miss that."

"Me too."

"And now here we are, the grandparents all of a sudden," he said.

"It wasn't all of a sudden, but it did happen fast when they started dropping like flies, one after the other. And Laura and Shane, too."

"They all found their ideal mates. I couldn't be any happier with how it worked out for them."

"Not to mention, they all came home."

"Thank goodness for that." Big Mac reached for the small wrapped package he'd stashed under his pillow before bed and plopped it down in front of her.

"What's that?"

"The first of your anniversary gifts."

"Mac! We said we weren't doing gifts!"

"We say that every year, and every year we do gifts. And besides, this year is extra special."

"Every year is extra special."

"Open your present."

Looking over her shoulder, he noted the slight tremble in her hands as she pulled the ribbon and paper off the blue velvet box.

"Mac," she said with a gasp, recognizing the distinctive Tiffany blue. "What've you done?"

"Open it." He'd been anticipating this moment for months as he went back and forth with the folks at Tiffany to get it just right. And judging by her gasp of shock, he'd gotten it just right.

"Mac... *Oh my God*, are you *kidding me?*" Holding the velvet box, she sat up in bed, her hand over her mouth as tears filled her gorgeous eyes.

He sat up, too, took the box from her, retrieved the ring and slid it onto her finger.

Her hand trembled as she held it out in front of her for a better look. "It's too much! My God!"

"It's four carats, one for every decade we've spent together, and it's the least of what you deserve for putting up with me that long."

"Putting up with you? Is that what you think I've done?"

"Sometimes," he said with a smile.

"Mac...all these years later, you still think you lured me away from some grandiose life for something lesser here, and that's not the case at all. I've been exactly where I wanted to be every day that I lived here with you."

"You could've had anyone."

"*You* could've had anyone."

"I chose you. My heart chose you. I'll never forget the first time I laid eyes on you and knew it was you. I just *knew*."

She took his hand and brought it to rest over her heart. "My heart chose you, too. It still does. Every day."

Smiling, he used their joined hands to tug her closer to him. "We've got a lot of celebrating to do today. What do you say we get this party started?"

"What do you have in mind?"

"What do I always have in mind when you're in bed with me?"

She laughed and reached for him. "At least you're predictable."

Overwhelmed by love for her, he pressed his lips against her neck. "Thanks for spending forty years with me, Lin. You've made my whole life just by being here."

"Same goes, my love."

CHAPTER 3

Mac McCarthy Junior woke on that cold winter day to the distinctive sound of retching coming from the master bathroom. He was up and out of bed before his brain had time to catch up with his body. Maddie was sick again, and he couldn't bear to listen to her suffer.

Though she'd told him before she didn't want him anywhere near her when she was puking, he defied her orders and went in to hold her hair back while she dry heaved, flushing the toilet for her when she was done.

"Mac," she said between waves of nausea, "go away."

"Not happening. It's my fault you're sick, so you have to let me help you."

"It's not your fault, and I don't want you seeing me like this."

"Aren't we past that by now? Don't ask me to pretend I can't hear you throwing up."

She moaned and rested her face on the arm she had propped on the toilet.

Mac released her hair and went to wet a washcloth with cool water. Her eyes remained closed while he got her to lift her head so he could wipe her face and mouth. Then he encouraged her to lean on him rather than the toilet.

"It's so gross. Who wants to see his wife like this?"

"I do. I want to see my wife every minute of every day, and I don't care what she looks like."

"Or what she smells like?"

He nuzzled her neck. "She always smells delicious."

That drew a grunt of laughter from her. "Sure she does."

"Is it over for now?"

"I think so."

"Let's get you back to bed for a while." He helped her up and kept his hands on her hips while she brushed her teeth and rinsed her mouth. Then he lifted her into his arms and carried her back to bed. That she rested her head on his shoulder rather than protesting him carrying her indicated how lousy she felt.

He laid her gently on the bed, pulled the comforter up and over her and then got back into bed with her.

She shivered violently. "Freezing."

"Let me warm you up."

Maddie curled up to him, and Mac wrapped his arms around her, tucking her in as close to him as he could get her. "I'm sorry you're suffering so much this time around."

"It's fine. Whatever I have to do."

Mac rubbed small circles on her back. "How're the boobs feeling?"

"Awful. They're so sore."

He kissed her forehead. "My poor baby."

"I refuse to think of myself as anything other than a lucky mommy who's getting another chance."

"Still, it sucks that you feel so crappy."

"This too shall pass, and at the end of it, we'll have a healthy, beautiful baby. I hope."

He hated that she felt the need to add those two little words at the end. "Victoria said there's no reason to believe we have anything to worry about this time."

"We didn't think we had anything to worry about last time, and I went around telling everyone how I didn't really want to be pregnant, how it was all a big comic accident."

"It *was* a comic accident, and no one thought you wanted to lose him, Maddie. Not for one second did anyone think that."

"I like to think I've learned my lesson just the same."

They were quiet for a long time, with only the pinging of icy snow against the windows marking the silence.

"Do you think you'll feel up to going tonight?"

"Even if I don't, I'm going. Wouldn't miss it. Besides, we don't need everyone speculating as to why I'm sick all the time."

In light of what'd happened the last time, they'd agreed to keep the news to themselves for a few months. However, with Maddie so sick, the people closest to them were beginning to wonder what was up. "Let them speculate. We'll tell them when we're ready to."

"The day he's born?" she asked with a laugh.

It was good to hear her laugh, even if she was being sarcastic. "Maybe a little before then."

"What'll we name him?"

She'd been reluctant to talk too much about the baby that was due next summer, so he took it as a good sign when she asked about a name.

"I'm thinking Malcolm John the Third has a nice ring to it."

"We can't call him Mac. We've got too many Macs as it is."

"A family can never have too many Macs," he said.

She rolled her eyes. "That's what you think."

"We'll call him Malcolm. Why not? It's a good name. His friends will call him Mal. I like that."

"I like it, too. What if he is a *she?*"

"Since there's no way in hell she's going to be born during a tropical storm the way Hailey was, we'll have to come up with something for a girl that isn't the name of a storm."

"We've got plenty of time."

"Go back to sleep for a while, hon. I'll get up with the kids."

"You're the best husband I've ever had," she murmured.

"I'd better be the only husband you ever have, Mrs. McCarthy."

"Mmm, no one else but you."

That was all he needed to hear. Someday they'd be celebrating their fortieth anniversary. He had absolutely no doubt about that.

*

In Providence, Adam McCarthy woke to the sound of sobs coming from the bathroom in the hotel room he'd shared with his fiancée, Abby Callahan. Hearing her heartbroken sounds reminded him of the disastrous day they'd endured yesterday when Abby had been diagnosed with something neither of them had ever heard of—polycystic ovary syndrome.

At least they now knew why, despite a year of nearly constant effort, they had yet to conceive the child they both wanted so badly. And now it was quite possible they never would, thanks to a silent but virulent disorder that would require lifelong management.

Abby had been despondent since hearing the devastating news, and Adam was still trying to process what it meant. After she cried herself to sleep the night before, he'd spent hours on the Internet and had come away terrified for both of them. Conceiving a baby was now the least of their concerns, with the possibility of diabetes, cancer, heart disease and other life-threatening illnesses looming over her.

He got up to knock on the bathroom door. "Abs? Let me in, honey."

"No."

"Abby…please. I need you." After more than a year together, he knew what to say to get her attention, and she was a sucker for him when he needed her. Today was no different. The lock on the door popped open, and he had to suppress a gasp when he saw the ravages of grief and despair etched into her gorgeous face. He put his arms around her. "Come here, honey."

She shook her head and pushed him away. "No."

His Abby, the woman he loved more than he'd ever loved anyone in his life, never said no to him. And she never pushed him away. Placing his hands on her shoulders so she couldn't turn away, he said, "Baby, listen to me. We're going to deal with this together. We'll get the information we need. We'll find the best doctors in the country, and we'll fight it together."

She shook her head. "No, we won't."

"What do you mean?"

"I won't subject you to this. You want children, not a barren wife who'll have male-pattern baldness and hair in places it doesn't belong, not to mention cancer and other hideous things." She shook her head adamantly. "This is *not* your problem."

Adam stared at her as if she were someone he'd never met before. *This* Abby was someone he didn't recognize. "You're not thinking clearly today—"

"I'm thinking very clearly, and you're young enough to find someone else—"

He put his hand over her mouth to stop her from saying something that couldn't be unsaid—or unheard. "Stop. Just stop that right now. There is no one else in this world for me. Only you. And you can push me away and reject me and tell me you don't love me anymore, but I'm not going anywhere."

Tears poured down her cheeks as she shook her head. "You don't know what you're signing on for."

"I already signed the papers." He reached for her left hand and touched the engagement ring he'd put there months ago.

"We're not married yet. Nothing says we have to go through with it."

"I'm going to pretend you didn't say that. I'm going to pretend you're not trying to push me away because something has happened that we didn't see coming. I'm going to pretend you'd let me get away with this shit if the shoe were on the other foot. If I pretend all that, I won't be tempted to remind you that you love me and you made a commitment to me and you owe me better than this, regardless of what any doctors might have to say."

Tears streamed down her face. "It's not fair to you, Adam."

"Neither is you reneging on promises you made to me."

"I'd never renege on those promises under normal circumstances, but this is too much to ask of anyone, especially someone like you, who could have any woman—"

He'd heard more than enough, so he stifled her protests the only way he could think of, by yanking her into his embrace and kissing her until he was all but certain she had forgotten that she'd been trying to push him away. Moving slowly and carefully, he backed her out of the bathroom and eased her onto the bed, coming down on top of her without breaking the kiss.

When her arms encircled his neck, the tension that had gathered in Adam's chest began to ease ever so slightly. "I love you," he whispered gruffly when they finally came up for air many minutes later. "I love you and only you. I love you in good times, bad times, healthy times, sick times and every other minute in between. My love is not conditional on you being perfect. It's not conditional on you being able to bear children. It's not conditional on anything other than you loving me back, and until about five minutes ago, I thought you loved me as much as I love you."

"I do, *but*—"

He kissed her again. "No buts, no conditions, no nothing but you and me staring this thing down together, no matter what might happen. And P.S., the doctors didn't say having babies was hopeless. They said it would take some doing. So we'll do what we've got to do, no matter what it is, and we will get through this and every other goddamned thing that comes our way, because I'm not going anywhere and neither are you. I'm sorry to say you're stuck with me."

"What if I go bald and grow a beard?"

"Then I'll kiss your sweet bald head and teach you how to shave."

"Adam...I'm serious."

"So am I. Do you think I care if something you can't help happens to you? Do you think I'll love you only when you're young and beautiful?"

"I could get really heavy." She'd put on a few pounds in the last year that he knew she was stressed about.

"That's just more of you to love."

"You say that now..."

"I say that forever. In fact, we're getting married New Year's Eve." He decided that as he said the words. "No more delays, no more waffling, no more of anything other than you and me married. You've got your dress, and everyone will be home for the holidays. It's on."

"Adam, you're just saying that—"

"Because I want to be married to you more than I want anything in this world."

"You're awfully rude this morning."

"Likewise, my love. It's awfully rude of you to think I'm going to run for the hills at the first sign of trouble."

"This isn't just trouble. It's a life sentence."

"If that's how you'd like to view our marriage..."

"That's not what I meant, and you know it."

"I do know, and a far worse life sentence for me would be life without you. So don't condemn me to that by thinking I can't handle what's ahead, no matter what it may be. I can handle it as long as I have you and we have each other. Everything else is secondary to that."

She released a deep, shuddering breath marked by the hitches that came from hours of crying. "You're sure about this?"

He kissed her again. "I've never been more sure about anything in my life. Ever. Remember that first week we spent together?"

"As if I could ever forget it." She traced the outline of the Gansett Island tattoo on his bicep.

"And when we were apart, when I was back in New York for those interminable weeks…I thought I'd die from missing you. I couldn't wait to get everything wrapped up there so I could come home to you. I still feel that way, every day when I go to work on someone's malfunctioning computer. Every minute I'm away from you, I'm counting down until I can get home to you. There is nothing, and I do mean *nothing*, that could make me not want to go home to you, Abs. Not even something I can hardly pronounce."

"Polycystic ovary syndrome."

"Not even that." He kissed her again, lingering when she responded enthusiastically, the way she usually did. That gave him hope that he could eventually disabuse her of the idea that he couldn't handle this. "So New Year's Eve… It's on, yes? I'll take care of everything. All you'll have to do is show up looking gorgeous as usual."

"Okay."

If her one-word response lacked enthusiasm, well, he had eleven days to work on that before they exchanged vows. He was determined to be everything she needed and to stand by her no matter what might come their way.

*

In Nashville, Tennessee, Evan McCarthy woke to the supreme pleasure of his fiancée, Grace, in his arms after she'd surprised him on the final night of his three-week tour with superstar Buddy Longstreet. Evan's single, "My Amazing Grace," written to honor the love of his life, was charting in the top three on all the industry lists, which was a surprise to no one but him, apparently.

Buddy said he'd known the song would be a smash hit the first time he heard it, and last night, after their show, Buddy had taken him aside with yet another plea to continue pursuing music. "You'd be a fool to go back to your studio on the island when you have a song in the top three, Evan," Buddy had said in his typically blunt way. "This is your moment. *Carpe diem.*"

Buddy's words had upended his plans to rush home to Grace and Island Breeze Records the minute the last show ended. And then Grace had further upended his plans, in the best possible way, by being naked in his bed when he returned to the hotel. Best. Surprise. Ever. He'd missed her so much, even though he'd talked to her several times a day, FaceTimed with her every night and engaged in an unseemly amount of phone sex.

There was nothing, absolutely *nothing*, like the real thing when it came to his amazing Grace. He was a little ashamed of how rough he'd been with her last night after missing her so desperately while he was away. But she'd been right there with him, encouraging him to take anything and everything he needed from her.

He ran his hand over the soft skin on her back, touching her because he could. If you'd told him a couple of years ago that he'd be so in love with one woman that he'd turn his back on stardom, he might've suggested you have your head examined. But now that he had her, everything else had taken a backseat to their life together. And it would continue to, he decided right in that moment.

Even Buddy's promises of stardom like he'd once dreamed of weren't enough to lure him away from Grace or the home they'd made together on the island. It wasn't enough to turn his back on a year of hard work building the studio or getting it up and running. The weeks on stage had reminded him of a time in his life when *everything* was an epic struggle.

Having Grace back in his arms was a reminder that life with her was as easy as breathing. No comparison, no debate, no decision. She was what he wanted. He wanted her more than he wanted bright lights and big cities. He wanted her more than he wanted fame or fortune or anything that didn't include being with her every day.

As he had that thought, one of her big brown eyes popped open. When she saw him there, her smile lit up her face. "Favorite face to wake up to."

He loved the sleepy, sexy sound of her voice in the morning. He loved being the first person she spoke to every day. He loved being the last one she touched each night. Tracing the outline of her precious face, he said, "Me, too. Best face in the whole wide world."

"I was afraid you wouldn't be happy to see me here."

"*What?* Why would you think that for one second?"

"Because this is your world, not mine. I felt like I might be intruding."

"Grace… My world is you and me together in our little place on the island. This," he said, gesturing to the fancy suite Buddy had arranged for him, "is not my world."

"It could be," she said tentatively. "People are talking. You've got a huge hit with the song, and I read online that you're the next big thing. The Grand Ole Opry even wants you!"

"So what?"

Her eyes nearly bugged out of her head. "*So what?* Are you *insane?* This is what you've worked for your whole life! And you don't care?"

"I don't care."

"It's the Grand. Ole. *Opry. Evan.*"

"The Opry ain't got nothing on you, babe."

"What does that mean?"

How to explain what he didn't understand himself? "I love the music. You know I do. It's in my DNA, the same way my family is. It's who I am."

"It's what you need to be happy."

He shook his head. "Not anymore, Gracie. *You're* what I need to be happy, and I can't bear to be away from you for weeks at a time. These last few weeks were excruciating."

"They were for me, too, but we got through it, didn't we?"

"This time. If I stay on this path, I'll be gone more than I'll be home. That's not how I want to live. I don't want to live without you by my side every day, with weeks at a time apart. I can't handle it."

"I've been thinking." She pursed her lips the way she did when she had something on her mind. It was one of many adorable things he loved about her.

"What've you been thinking about?"

"I could sell the pharmacy."

He was shaking his head from the word *sell.* "No way. That's *your* dream, and it matters every bit as much as my dreams do."

"Hear me out before you say no."

Only because she had something she needed to get off her chest did he sigh and relax into the pillows, prepared to listen and then say no again.

"It's the only pharmacy on the island, which makes it extremely valuable. Someone will buy it. We'd make money on the sale, even after I pay off what I still owe the Golds."

"And what will you do with yourself while I'm on the road?"

"I'll be with you. That's more important to me than anything else, even the pharmacy."

He reached up to caress her sweet face, staring at her because he could, because he'd missed her so damned much while he'd been away from her.

"Evan. You're staring. Say something."

"I love you so much. Never in my wildest dreams did I imagine anything like this for myself, and I've had some pretty wild dreams."

Her face softened into a smile that made her eyes sparkle. "I feel the exact same way about you. I don't want to spend weeks away from you, but I also don't want you to wake up someday and wish you'd taken the next step to find out what happened after you finally had a hit record. We're young, unencumbered—except for the pharmacy—and free to do whatever we want for a few years until we have kids that we'll want to raise at home with our family. I could even hire a pharmacist to run the place for me for a few years, and you could pay Josh to run the studio. We'd have jobs to come home to when we're ready."

"You're serious about this."

"I'm so serious. You can't *not* do this, Ev. You have to go for it. Our song is on the *charts.* Don't you want to know what happens next?"

"Sort of." He'd never admit how often he'd had that very thought, but knowing it wasn't an option for them, he hadn't allowed it to flourish. Until now.

"Will you think about it?"

"Yeah, I will, since you make it all sound so easy."

"I don't think it'll be easy, but it *is* doable. I spent a lot of time thinking about it while you were gone, and at some point, it occurred to me that we're both self-employed. There's no reason we can't make some changes that'll allow us to take this ride together rather than apart. I don't want to be apart from you."

"I don't want that either. It's hell."

"If I'm with you, then you can relax and enjoy it and come home to me every night rather than an empty hotel room."

"I'm very, very tempted, my amazing Grace."

"Let's do it, Evan. Let's just do it."

He shifted so he was on top of her and gathered her into his arms as he entered her slowly and carefully, knowing she had to be sore after the voracious night they'd spent together. But no matter when he reached for her, she was ready for him, which was another thing he adored about her.

Sighing with pleasure, she raised her hips in encouragement. "You took me quite literally."

Chuckling, he kissed her neck and nibbled at her skin. "Oh, so you didn't mean *this* when you said we should *do it?*"

Smiling up at him, Grace wrapped her arms around him as he lost himself in her. She'd given him a lot to think about, but right now, all he could think about was her and how amazing it felt to make love to her.

CHAPTER 4

After a leisurely breakfast of scrambled eggs, bacon and toast, Linda saw to the dishes while Mac went outside to shovel snow off the deck. She rinsed soapy water off her hands, revealing the dazzling new ring from her husband. He was still bowling her over, like he had from the beginning when he'd swept her off her feet with his certainty that they belonged together. It had taken her a little longer to catch up with him, but once she had, she'd never looked back.

She kept an eye on the weather and the whitecaps in the Salt Pond, hoping against hope that Evan, Grace, Adam and Abby would make it back to the island in time for the party she and Mac weren't supposed to know about tonight. If the ferries were even still running, the kids faced a rough ride home, not that high seas fazed her island-born sons. The girls might not like it, though.

Thinking of rough seas had her remembering her first trip to Gansett Island, which still ranked as one of the worst ferry rides she'd ever endured. Poor Mac had been convinced that she'd never speak to him again after she'd gotten sick on the boat.

She poured a second cup of coffee and took it with her to turn on the Christmas tree lights and sit in the rocking chair that overlooked the deck so she could watch Mac shovel. Even after all these years, she never got tired of looking at him. And she remembered that first trip to Gansett as if it were yesterday.

Murmuring sweet words of comfort, he'd held the hair back from her face while she retched over the side. "We're almost there. I can see the bluffs now."

They'd taken a midafternoon boat, and he'd been riding high since closing on the marina earlier in the day, proclaiming himself the "poorest future rich man" she'd ever meet.

After meeting him the day before and being steamrolled by his persuasive charm, she'd expected him to be less appealing today. But he'd been so excited about the marina he now owned and so thrilled to take her to the island that his appeal from yesterday was eclipsed by the excitement of today.

She felt like she was raining on his parade by getting sick, but he was endlessly patient with her.

"Happens to a lot of people the first few times they make the trip," he said.

"If you say so," she muttered.

"A few more minutes, and we'll be good to go."

"And then we have to get home."

"One thing at a time."

She kept meaning to tell him he shouldn't be holding her so close or stroking her back and hair so tenderly one day after they met, but she couldn't seem to muster the wherewithal to protest, not when he smelled fantastic and made her feel so safe despite the heaving seas.

"This is all my fault. I wanted you to see the island so badly that I never gave a thought to what the seas would be like today."

"It doesn't bother you?"

"Nah," he said with a chuckle. "I kinda like it."

"Figures." Despite how miserable she felt, she didn't want to be a downer on his big day, so she tried to rally, standing upright only to have her head spin.

"Easy, honey." He held her close to him so she wouldn't topple over. "Hang on to me. I've got you."

Oh, he was something, this Malcolm John McCarthy. Handsomest guy she'd ever laid eyes on, with rich, dark hair and eyes so blue they took her breath away. Yes, she'd noticed him, too, standing next to his equally attractive brother on the porch of Frank's house. The way he'd overwhelmed her on their walk yesterday afternoon should've been off-putting. Any other guy who'd tried to pull such nonsense with her would've been sent packing. But there was something different about this guy—and his nonsense. Though she'd only just met him, she'd believed every outrageous word he said.

She might live to regret that, but for right now—seasickness notwithstanding—she was determined to enjoy the moment and not ruin his big day.

"Few more minutes," he said in that soothing tone that drew her attention from her queasy stomach to focus on the deep, rich sound of his voice.

Closing her eyes, she breathed through the nausea, focusing on the scent of his cologne.

"Look," he said. "There's my island."

Linda opened her eyes and blinked the rugged coastline into focus, committing her first view of the island to memory. Wild, untamed, beautiful… Her heart fluttered with excitement and anticipation. With the island acting as a buffer for the wind, the seas calmed, and so did her stomach.

The ferry cut through the water, heading for a harbor that she could now see through the fog.

"Come on." He took her by the hand to head for the stairs. They were on their way down to where they'd left his truck when the crew made an announcement that car owners needed to return to their vehicles. Clearly, Mac had done this a few times and already knew the routine.

He was like a little boy on Christmas, vibrating with eagerness as the ferry backed into port and the first cars began to drive onto the island. His fingers tapped impatiently on the steering wheel.

Linda felt the impatience coming off him in waves until the car in front of them finally rolled forward.

"Every single thing you buy or eat or drink on this island comes off these boats." He pointed to pallets sealed in plastic that lined the ferry's cargo area. "They even bring the mail."

"From what I see, a lot of beer gets consumed here."

"Oh yeah. You know it."

"By you?" she asked with a smile.

Winking at her, he said, "I'll never tell."

They drove off the boat onto the island, and Linda's excitement faded slightly at the sight of the town, such as it was—two hotels, a few shops, a restaurant here and there, but not much of anything else.

"That's The Beachcomber, which is a restaurant and hotel," Mac said of the huge white building that served as the heart of "downtown" Gansett. "And that one there," he said, pointing to a weathered Victorian-style building, "is the Sand & Surf. I've gotten to know the owners, Russ and Adele Kincaid, and their daughter, Sarah. Good people. They've owned the Surf for almost ten years, and they love it here."

"They live here year-round?"

"Yep. About four hundred people do, believe it or not. We've even got a K-through-twelve school out here with twenty-five students."

She noted his use of the word *we*, as if he were already firmly entrenched in the local community.

"So we came in at South Harbor, which is a manmade harbor."

"How does man make a harbor?"

"Did you see the breakwater made of huge rocks?"

"I did."

"That was built over a period of two years. The idea was to make it so the ferries landed in town, where most of the businesses are. My place is over in North Harbor on the other side of the island. North Harbor is also called the Great Salt Pond, and it's well protected from the elements. I'd much rather be over there than in town, especially when it's storming."

As he drove, Linda took in the sights. She noticed a small grocery store, an even tinier post office and a place called Gold's, which she realized was a pharmacy as they went by it.

"That's the island's only liquor store," Mac said, pointing to a red building. "They do an extremely good business there."

"I imagine they do," Linda said, chuckling.

"I would've wanted in on that business if they didn't already have a liquor store here."

"From what you've said, the business you have is going to keep you plenty busy enough."

"It is, and before we get there, I just want you to know… Don't look at it the way it is today. Look at it and see the possibilities."

"Okay…"

"It's in pretty rough shape, but I have a plan, and I'm going to make it happen. I swear to you, Linda. I'm going to make a go of that place."

She found his fierce determination and ambition extremely appealing. When these qualities were combined with his handsome good looks, they made for quite an overwhelming young man. None of the other boys she'd dated were anything like him. They were interested in partying and getting laid. Mac was thinking of his future.

"Do you think less of me because I never went to college?" he asked. "You can be honest."

"I was actually just thinking how different you are—in a good way—from all the other boys I know. None of them think beyond next weekend."

His hand tightened on the steering wheel. "I bet a lot of boys want to be with you."

"But which one am I with today?"

The smile he directed her way told her he liked her answer.

"If I have my way, you'll never date anyone else ever again."

"Well, tell me how you really feel."

"I just did."

His self-confidence was another thing she found wildly attractive about him. He put it right out there and didn't hold back. He didn't play games or act like a fool the way so many twenty-year-old boys did. No, this twenty-year-old was already a man and fully in control of his own life.

"So here's the marina." He drove around deep potholes in the parking lot and brought the truck to a stop outside a barn-shaped building with a sagging roof, peeling paint and broken windows. Next to it, two smaller buildings were in similar disrepair. Beyond the buildings, an equally dilapidated pier slanted precariously in the middle.

The Great Salt Pond seethed with whitecaps as the wind whipped across the water, making Linda's stomach turn at the thought of the ride home later.

"Like I said, it's not much. Yet. But it will be. I'll be working until the first snow to renovate the buildings and then, in the spring, I'm going to rebuild the main dock. We'll be ready to open for business by next June."

"It's..." Linda didn't know what to say.

"I'm crazy," he said with a sigh. "It's okay. You can say it. It's nothing my dad hasn't already said."

He sounded so dejected that Linda leapt immediately to his defense. How dare anyone, even his own father, crap on his dreams? "It's going to be beautiful."

Brightening, he asked, "You think so? Really?"

"I know so. The place has good bones. Sure, it needs some work, but I can see the potential." She released her seat belt. "Show me around."

He met her at the front of the truck, holding out his hand to her.

As she joined her hand with his, she noticed his fierce expression. "What?"

"What you said, about seeing the potential... That means so much to me. Thank you for saying that."

"I mean it. With a little TLC, it could be magnificent."

He raised his free hand to stroke her cheek, setting off all sorts of fireworks inside her. "I think *you're* magnificent."

Linda had never thought of herself as the kind of girl who swooned, but damn if he didn't make her feel capable of such theatrics. "Thank you. You're quite magnificent yourself, with all your lofty dreams and ambition."

"I'm glad you think so. I was afraid after the way I came on to you yesterday that I'd never see you again."

"It takes more than a little intensity to scare me off."

"What would scare you off? Tell me so I never do it."

"Making promises you have no intention of keeping would scare me off."

"I'll never promise you anything I can't deliver. What else?"

"A wandering eye would scare me off."

"Why would I look at anyone else when I have you to look at?"

He said this as if it was the most preposterous thing he'd ever heard, and she lost a tiny piece of her heart to him right then and there.

"What else?" he asked.

"I can't think of anything else off the top of my head."

"Let me know if you think of any other deal breakers."

"I will."

Mac released her hand to withdraw a set of keys from his pocket and unlocked the door of the main building. They stepped inside, and he flipped a switch on the wall. Nothing happened. "Aw, come on. The power was supposed to be turned on today. Hang on a second."

While Linda stayed by the door, he ventured into the building. She heard rustling before a flashlight beam cut across the darkness.

He went to another set of doors to unlock and open them. They were huge garage doors that opened most of one side of the building to the pier. "There. Now at least you can get a sense of the place."

She saw dust and dirt and a lime-green countertop and spiders that scurried out of the light. Linda moved a little closer to Mac.

"Let me guess," he said, sliding an arm around her. "Spiders will run you off."

"They aren't my favorite thing."

"I'll get rid of them. Don't worry."

"What's behind the counter?"

"Nothing right now, but I was thinking someday it might be a restaurant. We could sell clam chowder and hot dogs and burgers to the customers."

"And clam cakes and fried clams and all things Rhode Island and New England."

"Yes," he said with another of those wide smiles.

"My mom makes the most incredible sugar donuts. I bet you'd sell a million of them in a place like this."

"My mouth is already watering."

She held out her hand to ask for the flashlight.

He gave it to her.

Braving the spiders and other creepy things, she moved toward the counter, going around behind it to check out the available space. She could envision a full kitchen back there as well as tables and chairs on the other side of the counter where people could sit and eat.

"What's back there?" she asked, pointing the beam toward a corridor.

"Go take a look."

"Only if you come with me."

"I'm right behind you." He put his hands on her shoulders, providing immediate comfort.

In the hallway, she discovered a small room with a bed frame and nothing else. "Is that why you have the mattress?" The back of his truck was full to capacity with things he'd brought from Providence. "You're going to live here?"

"Yep."

"For how long?"

"Until I open and start making some money. Then I'll rent something in town. But for now, this is home sweet home."

"It's, um, kinda rustic."

His bark of laughter made her smile. "I prefer the word *cozy* to *rustic*."

"You're going to freeze here in the winter."

"No, I won't. I've got good heaters and lots of warm clothes. I'll be fine."

Linda shivered just thinking about spending a winter in a creaky, saggy building that was also home to an army of spiders. "What're you thinking about doing with the other buildings?"

"One of them will be the dock office and the other a gift shop, maybe." He took her by the hand to lead her back into the main part of the building. "How're you feeling?"

"Fine, now that I'm back on land."

"So you might be up for a late lunch?"

"I could eat."

"Let me unload the truck real quick, and then there's a place you've got to see. They've got a *thousand* painted oars on the walls. You'll love it."

"Sounds good to me."

*

Mac came in from shoveling snow, clomping his boots on the mat inside the sliding glass door. In the summer, they left that door open most of the time to let the sea air in through the screen. This time of year, they kept it closed except for when he went out to remove the heavy snow from the deck.

"It's freaking freezing out there."

Seeing that he was dripping all over her wood floor, Linda got up to fetch a towel.

"Thanks, babe. Sorry I'm making a mess."

"It's okay. At least the deck won't collapse."

"Remember that?"

"How could I forget?" The first winter they'd lived in this house, they found out the hard way that keeping the snow from accumulating on the deck was critical to keeping the deck attached to the house. "Most awful sound I ever heard."

"It was the sound of more money down the drain and more work."

"Ah yes, those were the days of two money pits—the marina and this house," she said.

"Hard times, but the best of times, too."

"I was just thinking about the first day you brought me here."

He wiped his wet hair with the towel before he used it to mop up the mess on the floor. "When you got seasick and then they canceled the ferries? I thought for sure you'd be done with me forever after that day."

"It was a great day."

"I've never forgotten the look on your face when Carolina's dad told us they'd stopped running the ferries and you realized you were stuck here with me for the night." He laughed at the memory. "I swear you thought I'd arranged that so you'd have to spend the night."

"Still not convinced that you didn't."

"I wasn't that clever."

"You were the most clever boy I ever met. You still are."

"But I wasn't *that* clever. It never occurred to me that they'd cancel the boats. That was the first time the ferry schedule got in the way of my plans."

"But not the last." Linda eyed the whitecaps in the Salt Pond. "I sure do hope the kids can get here later."

"The boats are still running, as far as I know. If they aren't, Slim will get them here. He's due back later today."

"Not so sure I want my kids flying in this weather, either."

Mac kissed her forehead. "Try not to worry. They'll get here."

She put her arms around his waist and rested her head on his chest. "Remember that first night together at the marina?"

"How could I ever forget?"

CHAPTER 5

Did he remember? In the shower, warming up after spending an hour in the cold, shoveling snow, Mac recalled that long-ago afternoon. He and Linda had arrived at the ferry landing planning to take the five o'clock boat back to the mainland only to encounter a sign that said, "Ferries canceled until tomorrow."

His heart had sunk when he thought about her telling him she wouldn't spend the night on his island. Now she had no choice.

"Oh Lord," Linda said. "What now?"

Determined to put a positive spin on the unfortunate turn of events, Mac said, "Now we find you a hotel room." He'd spend money he didn't have to ensure her comfort.

She eyed him shrewdly. "Neither of us can afford a hotel room."

"It's okay. I've got it covered."

"Mac, we can stay at the marina. We'll make it work."

"Oh, um, well…" He ran his fingers through his hair, torn with indecision. Though she was trying to be helpful, he hadn't missed her freak-out over the spiders. They freaked him out, too, and getting rid of them was at the top of his to-do list. But he wouldn't achieve complete eradication between now and bedtime. And the thought of spending a night in close quarters with her… He couldn't think about that or he might embarrass them both.

"I need to find a phone somewhere so I can tell my roommates what's happened," Linda said. "Otherwise they'll send the state police after me."

"I have a friend with a phone. Let's go see him."

He drove them to his new friend Ned Saunders's place and was relieved to see Ned's station wagon in the driveway. Bringing Linda with him, Mac knocked on Ned's door.

"Hey," Ned said, smiling when he came to the door. "Yer back. Wondered if we'd see ya round here again."

"Told ya I'd be back, and you're looking at the official owner of McCarthy's Gansett Island Marina as of this morning."

"Congratulations."

"Thanks. This is my friend Linda. She came over with me for the day, and now the ferries are canceled. I wondered if she might use your phone to let her roommates know she's staying."

"Sure thing. Come in."

Ned showed Linda to the phone, and she thanked him as he blushed profusely.

While she made her call, Ned said to Mac, "Pretty gal ya got there."

"I'm going to marry her," Mac said, keeping his gaze trained on Linda as she talked to her friend.

"How long ya known her?"

"About twenty-four hours now."

Ned snorted with laughter. "Ya got big brass ones to go along with yer lofty ideas."

"Including the marina that almost everyone told me I shouldn't buy."

"Ya won't regret that. Prime real estate. Took a look at it myself, but it needed way more work than I wanted ta do."

"Glad you approve. My dad thinks I'm insane."

"Yer not. Not about the marina, anyway. That gal? Ya might have yer work cut out fer ya there. She's a fancy one."

"That's okay. I'm not afraid of a little hard work." Especially when Linda was the prize. "Who do I talk to about getting the power turned on at the marina?"

"Ya call the power company?"

"Yeah, they were supposed to start my service today, but so far nothing."

"I know a guy there. I'll call fer ya."

"Thanks, Ned. I appreciate all your help."

"T'aint no big deal."

"It is to me."

Linda ended her call and rejoined them.

"All set?" Mac asked. Though he felt bad that he hadn't been able to keep his promise to get her home tonight, he wasn't at all sorry that she had to spend the night with him. Not one bit sorry.

"All set. The girls were glad to hear from me. They said they definitely would've called the state police if I didn't call." This was said with a smile that made Ned chuckle.

"Smart gals," Ned said. Using his thumb to point to Mac, he said, "This one's got some big ideas."

"So I've heard," Linda said with a smile for Ned.

Before she could get too cozy with Ned, Mac took her by the hand. "We've got to get going. Thanks again for the use of your phone."

"Anytime," Ned said as he saw them out. "Hope ta see ya again, Linda."

"Hope so, too. Thanks for the phone."

"My phone is yer phone."

"He is *so* cute and sweet," Linda said when they were back in Mac's truck.

He glared at her, making her giggle.

"Not as cute as you," she said.

"But he is sweeter? Is that what you're saying?"

"I never said those words."

Mac smiled at her witty comeback. "It's okay. I like him, too. He's been really nice to me since the first time I came over to check out the marina."

"What does he do?"

"He drives a cab, which is how I met him, and he's getting into some real estate deals, too. Nothing big, a few things here and there, but he knows this island inside and out. He's a good friend to have."

"You're really settling in here," she said, gazing out the passenger window. The sun was a ball of fire in the late-afternoon sky, promising a spectacular sunset.

"That's the plan." For the first time since he set eyes on the marina and saw his future laid out before him, he had a moment of remorse. The marina didn't look quite as shiny to him as it had before he met her. Now that he knew she was in the world, he wanted *her* more than he wanted the marina, more than he wanted anything.

How could one day change everything? He had absolutely no experience with a woman turning his world upside down. Yes, he'd had girlfriends—one of them had even been sort of serious for a while, until he realized she had totally different goals in life than he did. Ending it with her had made sense in light of that revelation. As much as he'd liked Diana, he hadn't *needed* her the way he already knew he could need Linda.

"Mac."

He already loved the way his name sounded coming from her. Glancing over at her, he raised a brow in inquiry.

"I was thinking that if it's okay with you, I could just stay at the marina with you tonight."

If it's okay with me? He wanted to laugh out loud at how okay that was with him.

"Before you let your mind wander, I'm not offering anything special."

He covered her hand with his, noting how his dwarfed hers. "Yes, you are. You're offering to spend a whole night with me. If all we do is talk, that's definitely something special."

"You're such a charmer," she said with a laugh. "I have to watch out for you."

"No, you don't. Anything that happens between us will be on your schedule. I'd wait forever for you."

"I don't know how you can say such things so soon."

"I was struck by lightning when I saw you with Joann yesterday. I've never felt anything like it, and I know, I absolutely *know*, that I belong with you and vice versa."

"Mac... You can't say that kind of stuff to me the day after we met."

"I said it to you the *day* we met. Nothing changed overnight. At least, not for me."

"We're far too young to be talking this way."

"My dad had my brother on the way when he was my age. Who says we're too young?"

"I do. I have to finish college and get a job and do things. And so do you. Look at what you've just taken on here with the marina. We're too busy to be making life plans."

"If my life plan includes you, I'm not too busy. I'll never be too busy."

"I have no idea what to say to you when you talk this way."

"You don't have to say anything."

"You're sure you're never this forthright with women?"

"I'm sure. You're different."

"Why? Why am I so different?"

"I don't know. You just are. It's a feeling that I had when I first saw you. It was like how I felt when I first saw the marina. Certainty."

Taking the last turn before they reached the marina, he glanced over at her. "Have you ever felt that way about anything?"

"I'm trying not to feel that way about you."

"Why would you do something so foolish as try to deny the inevitable?"

"Because! Stuff like this doesn't happen to regular people. It's *preposterous*."

"That's a very fancy college word. Pre-pos-*terous*." Pointing to another large, dilapidated building on the hill above the marina, he said, "Speaking of preposterous, see that place?"

"What about it?"

"I want to buy it and turn it into a hotel. Not right away, but eventually."

She sighed deeply, making him wonder if he'd gone too far in sharing his hopes and dreams with her. But he'd never been one to hold back, and why would he start hedging now when the stakes were so high? "I can't keep up with you."

"Sure you can. You're more than equal to me. I bet between the two of us, we could turn this corner of the island into something quite spectacular."

"I'm an English major. What do I know about marinas and hotels?"

"About as much as I do, which is nothing. But I'm going to figure it out."

"I have no doubt that you'll make a spectacular success of anything you set your mind to."

He put the truck in park outside the main building at the marina and turned off the engine. "Anything?"

A sweet blush crept up her cheeks when she realized he'd included her in his list of anything he set his mind to.

Mac simply couldn't resist touching that flush of rosy color. "You're gorgeous, but of course you know that."

"No, I don't."

"Hasn't anyone ever told you that before?"

"Well, my mom and dad did, but they kind of have to."

"What's wrong with all the boys you've ever met?"

"They were boys."

Her meaning wasn't lost on him.

She leaned into the hand that he'd kept on her face. "They had nothing on you."

The compliment heated him from the inside, making him want her fiercely. Before he could do something stupid to mess things up, he said, "Let's go in. I need to spray the back room for spiders before bedtime."

Her shudder was a reminder of the monster task he had ahead of him at the marina—and in convincing her that she belonged with him. He couldn't very well talk her into spending her life in a spider-infested building with a sagging roof, broken glass and chipping paint. No, he needed to make this a showplace, worthy of a classy woman like her.

If he had been driven to succeed before he met her, now he was positively possessed with the desire to make a go of it, to offer her something she couldn't get anywhere else—him, his marina, his enormous desire to succeed. Somehow he had to make that enough for her, a woman who could have anyone she wanted.

He settled her in one of the few chairs the previous owner had left behind and went into the back room to spray for spiders, opening a window to vent the fumes. Earlier, he'd propped the mattress and the boxes he'd brought from home in the hallway, intending to spray before he took anything into the room.

With the sun setting over the Salt Pond, the view outside the room's single window took his breath away. After only three visits to the island before today, Mac already knew he'd never get tired of looking out at "his" pond, as he now thought of it. He unloaded an entire can of the spray in the small room, holding his breath the entire time. When he was finished, he shut the door, hoping the spray would do the trick to get rid of the spiders before the woman of his dreams had to sleep in there.

"How'd it go?" she asked when he returned to her.

"Score one for the good guys."

"We'll see about that."

"Have faith. I'll never let the spiders get you."

"Sorry to be such a baby today. Spiders have always freaked me out, but I had no idea I'd get seasick too."

"You're not a baby. Spiders are disgusting, and those seas were rough. That's why they canceled the ferries. So you see, it's not your fault you got sick."

"Always a charmer."

"I speak only the truth. Are you ready for some dinner?"

"If you are."

He went to the cooler he'd brought from home and retrieved two of the chicken sandwiches his mother had made to get him through his first day on the island. It had been her way of being supportive of his new endeavor, and he'd been touched by her kind gesture. "I have beer and water. What's your preference?"

"I'll have a beer."

Mac opened two bottles and handed one to her along with a sandwich. "Sorry it's not more fancy."

"This is perfect."

And it was. He'd never owned anything other than his old truck, and to sit inside *his* building—even if it was falling down around him—with a view of *his* pond and *his* woman sitting beside him... Life didn't get any better than this. "It is kind of perfect, but only because you're here with me. I'd be lonely here by myself."

"What'll you do all winter here by yourself?"

"Work and sleep."

"And what else?"

"That's it until I'm ready to open in the spring." He glanced over at her, watching her lips move as she took a sip of her beer. God, she was gorgeous. "Will you come visit me from time to time?"

"Maybe," she said with a coy smile.

His heart sank at the thought of all the college boys she'd be with every day. He couldn't possibly compete with them. In addition to being two hours by car and ferry from her, he couldn't really afford to go home very often. The thoughts, one on top of the other, depressed him profoundly.

"What's wrong?" she asked.

"Just thinking about obstacles."

"What obstacles?"

"The ones standing between you and me. College boys, for one thing."

She rolled her eyes. "No worries there. I haven't met one yet who did a thing for me."

"You haven't? Really?"

Shaking her head, she said, "What else?"

"Distance. That's a lot of water standing between where you're going to be and where I'm going to be."

"You're going to get a phone, right?"

"The minute I possibly can."

"And you'll use it to call me?"

"Every single day. Maybe twice a day."

"You can't afford that."

"I have my captain's license. I'm hoping to get some work taking charters, fishing trips. That kind of thing. I'll find a way to afford the phone, the calls, trips to see you whenever I can."

"When will you sleep?"

"I can sleep when I'm dead," he said with a teasing grin.

"Don't say things like that. I'm already having nightmares about you falling off that sagging roof and no one knowing it for days."

There was nothing she could've said that would've touched him more deeply at that particular moment. To know she cared enough to worry about him... "Nothing's going to happen to me. I don't want you to worry."

"I will worry."

He reached for her hand and loved the way she linked her fingers with his. "Don't go out with any of those college boys who'll be asking, you hear me?"

"I won't."

"You promise?"

"Yes, Mac, I promise."

Closing his eyes, he breathed a deep sigh of relief. "You know what this means, don't you?"

"I'm sure you're going to tell me."

"It means you're my girl, and I'm your…whatever you want me to be—boyfriend, fiancé, husband, you name it. I'm all yours."

She fanned her face dramatically. "It's getting warm in here."

Because he had to do something to stop himself from grabbing her and kissing her and trying to cajole her to do much more than kiss him, he leapt to his feet. "Let's go swimming. You brought a bathing suit, right?"

"Yes, but—"

"Great! Let's get changed and go to the beach."

"Mac—"

"You'll love it. I promise." Desperate times called for cold water, and he'd been told the Salt Pond was always cold, even in the summer. He directed her to the tiny bathroom across the hall from the bedroom, and after the door clicked shut behind her, he took a deep breath. "Slow down," he whispered. "Don't scare her off by acting crazy."

Mac was on fire for her, which she'd surely notice if he didn't get himself under control—quickly. He pulled off his shorts and boxers and put on his bathing suit, tucking his rampant erection into the netting. "Stop, stop, *stop*." Trying not to be hard for her was like trying not to breathe.

He'd nearly won the battle of wills with his libido when she stepped out of the dark hallway, wearing a red bikini. Dear God. And just that fast, his cock stood at full attention again.

She didn't help the situation one bit when she took a long, greedy look at his bare chest, seeming to like what she saw. Suddenly, his great idea to go swimming became the worst idea he'd ever had. Removing clothing with her around wasn't going to make anything better. It would only make everything worse.

Then she crossed the room to him, never taking her eyes off him as she moved.

"You have a lot of muscles," she said.

Mac groaned. "I'm trying to be a gentleman, but you're not making it easy."

She shocked the shit out of him when she laid her hand flat against his chest. "You're very handsome."

"Linda…"

Her hand dropped to her side, and he wanted to weep from the loss of her touch.

"Sorry. I'm not usually so forward."

"Please be forward. Touch me anytime you want to. I loved it." Blowing out another breath and seeking the equilibrium that had deserted him the second she touched him, he found two towels in one of the boxes and took hold of her hand. "Let's swim."

They walked around to the back of the marina, past the building he hoped to someday turn into a hotel, to a strip of sandy beach, where they left the towels and their sandals. Wading into the cool, refreshing water, she continued to hold his hand. He hoped she never let go.

When they were waist-deep, he looked over to see her gazing at the last remnants of the sun, a fireball of light heading for the horizon. "What're you thinking?"

"This place is beautiful."

"I couldn't agree more. I'm glad you think so, too."

"I can see why you fell in love with it."

"I can't wait to look at this view every day for the rest of my life." He dropped down into the water, bringing her with him to float on the surface. Over the last hour, the wind had dropped off considerably, and the gentle sway of the water soothed him.

A sense of rightness came over him. This was where he belonged. It was where she belonged, too. Maybe she didn't know it yet, but he hoped she would before too long.

"I have a confession to make," she said, breaking the comfortable silence.

"Do tell."

"I'm glad the ferries were canceled."

Smiling, he said, "Me, too." He drew her into his arms, gazing down at her, memorizing every detail of her gorgeous face.

She floated into his embrace, seemingly without reservation, linking her arms around his neck and her legs around his waist, looking up at him expectantly.

"Linda, I, um…"

With her hand on the back of his neck, she drew him into a kiss. The instant his lips connected with hers, all the restraint he'd been relying on during their day together shattered, and fierce need took over. He wasn't gentle or careful with her, the way a man should be with the woman he wanted to spend forever with.

She met every stroke of his tongue and every move of his body. Despite the chill of the water, the heat of her body scorched him as she rocked against him. He broke the kiss only to breathe.

"Holy shit," he whispered against her ear, making her shiver.

Her soft giggle flamed the fire burning hot and bright inside him.

"I, you…we…"

His stammering only made her laugh harder, so he kissed her again and again and again, until his lips were numb and his cock was so hard, he could barely stand the friction of her rocking against him. "Babe," he said, cupping her sweet ass, "we have to stop or we'll…"

"What will we do?" she asked in a husky, sexy whisper that traveled through him like a live wire.

"You know what we'll do, and I promised I'd behave if you came here with me."

"Promises are made to be broken," she said, her teeth clamping down on his earlobe.

Even during the worst of his hot and horny high school years, Mac had never lost control the way he was about to right now. Reluctantly, he moved them toward the shore, needing to put the brakes on this situation before they did something that couldn't be undone.

He guided her onto the beach and put a towel around her shoulders.

Maybe if he couldn't see her full breasts, he would refrain from touching them to determine whether they were as perfect as they looked in the bikini. Running the towel over his face, he took more deep breaths, trying to slow the pounding cadence of his heart. If he kept it up with the deep breathing, he'd probably hyperventilate.

"Mac?"

He lowered the towel to find her watching him warily.

"Are you mad or something?"

"*Mad?* No," he said with a short laugh. "I'm not mad. I'm *going* mad trying to behave myself with you."

"Oh."

"You really thought I was mad with you?"

"I didn't know."

"Sweetheart, I'm the opposite of mad. I'm crazy about you. I never want to stop kissing you and holding you and doing everything else with you. But I'm afraid you'll wise up and realize you could do so much better than the owner of a broken-down marina—"

"Stop." Her fingers on his lips electrified him. Would it always be this way when she touched him? "There's no one better than you."

When he started to shake his head, she took him by the face, looked him in the eyes and kissed him. "No one," she said again, more emphatically this time.

Sliding his arms around her, he fell into the kiss, falling deeper into infatuation and arousal and madness with every second she spent in his arms. Then the buzz of a motorbike on the nearby road reminded him of where they were. "Not here," he said gruffly, breaking the kiss to grab her hand and bring her with him to the marina, where he could kiss her in private.

CHAPTER 6

Linda scurried along with him, each of them carrying a towel back to the marina. Mac dropped his right inside the door and then took hers and dropped it on the floor.

"They'll never dry in a pile on the floor."

"I'll worry about that later. Hang on for one minute." Not sure what was about to happen, Mac went to the bedroom, where the scent of bug spray lingered, but not as strongly as before. He brought the mattress into the room and quickly made the bed with the sheets and comforter his mother had helped him buy last week.

Then, with his heart pounding and his mouth gone dry with nerves and desire, he went for Linda, took her by the hand and brought her into the room. "No more spiders," he said, hoping against hope that was true.

"It looks nice in here." She dropped his hand and went to sit on the bed. "Comfortable."

"It will be. Eventually."

"It is now." She lay back on the bed, putting her arms above her head in a leisurely stretch that put her breasts on full display and reignited the fire in his blood.

Mac swallowed hard, his hands rolling into fists at his sides.

"Are you going to join me?"

"Do you want me to?"

"Yes, Mac," she said, laughing, "I want you to."

His heart beat so hard and so fast that he began to worry he might pass out or something equally embarrassing as he lowered himself to the bed and reached for her. She came into his embrace like she'd been doing it forever. His leg slid between hers, and her hand landed on his chest.

"Hi there," she said, her smile lighting up her eyes.

He wanted to make her smile every day so he could watch her eyes light up like that. "Hey."

"How you doing?"

"Never been better. You?"

"Same here."

"Really?"

"Yes, Mac, really. Do you think you're the only one who's bowled over here?"

"I was sort of hoping it wasn't just me."

"It's not." She took his hand and placed it on her chest. "Feel that?"

Her heart beat wildly under his palm. "Yeah."

"That's because of you."

"I seem to be suffering from the same condition." He put her hand on his chest.

"Oh, so you are."

"My heart has never pounded like that for anyone else."

"No?"

He shook his head.

"Have there been many others?"

"A few here and there, one that might've been serious, but we wanted different things from life."

"What did she want?"

"Travel and adventure and a life far away from a remote island off the coast of Rhode Island."

"Were you sad when it ended?"

"For a while, but I'm over that now. How about you? Any serious boyfriends?"

"One in high school."

"What happened to him?"

"He joined the Peace Corps, and I haven't seen him in a couple of years."

"Do you miss him?"

"I did."

"Until when?"

"Until yesterday, when I met you, and now I can't seem to remember his face or the sound of his voice. I see only you. I hear only you."

A low groan escaped from Mac's tightly clenched jaw. "Is this real? Are you real?"

"It's real. It's so real."

"How am I going to take you home tomorrow when I want to keep you here with me forever?"

"Let's talk about that tomorrow. We have a lot of time between now and then."

"Not nearly enough." Then he was kissing her as if his life depended on her, and maybe it did. Maybe any chance he'd ever have to be truly happy came down to this tiny woman with the big personality, bright smile and dazzling eyes. All he knew was, he'd never felt anything remotely like he did when he kissed her.

She drove him mad with the sweet, sexy way she kissed him, her tongue stroking his and making him see stars as he tried to hold back, to save something for next time.

"Mac," she said breathlessly, "touch me. Don't be afraid. I won't break."

"I might," he said gruffly, making her laugh.

"No, you won't."

Keeping his gaze fixed on her face, he untied the top of her bikini and drew it down, revealing gorgeous breasts.

"Linda," he said on a long exhale as he watched her nipples harden before his eyes. "Sexiest girl I ever met."

She ran her fingers through his hair, drawing him down to her and then gasping when he drew the tight tip of her right breast into his mouth.

One taste of her and he was a goner, completely lost to her in every possible way.

*

The feel of her fingers sliding through his hair drew him out of the memory.

She sat on his lap, making him groan from the press of her bottom against his erection. "Whatever you're thinking about, it must be something good."

"I'm thinking about the red bikini."

"*Ahhhh.*"

"Remember that first night we spent together?"

"Do I ever! We drove each other insane."

"For months, we drove each other insane. I thought I was literally going to die from wanting you for all those months you made me wait."

"I did *not* make you wait! You made *me* wait!"

"I was trying to be honorable."

She snorted with laughter. "While we did almost everything *but…*"

"It was so hot. All of it."

"Mmm, and the phone calls." She fanned her face. "Speaking of hot."

"So hot. Every time the ferries have been canceled since that first night, I think of you and the red bikini and the back room at the marina."

"Don't forget the spiders."

"Just a few, but I got rid of them."

"I'll never forget the way I ached leaving you the next day," she said. "In the course of two days, I lost interest in school and my life in Providence and fell completely in love with you and your island."

"Took you long enough to say so."

"You're still holding a grudge about that?"

"I'll always hold a grudge about how long you made me wait to hear that you'd fallen as hard for me as I had for you."

"Three weeks, Mac. I waited *three weeks* to tell you that."

"Torture."

She laughed softly as he hugged her more tightly. "You were in the biggest rush."

"I knew what I wanted, and I was determined to get it—and you. Sometimes I wonder if your parents didn't resent me until the day they died for luring you out of school to my remote little island."

"They loved you."

"Not at first, they didn't."

"They always liked you. They just thought we were too young to make major life decisions."

"We were *way* too young at nineteen and twenty. I would've flipped my lid if any of our kids had done what we did."

"But there was no telling us that."

"Nope, and I don't regret anything we did. It was right for us."

"Yes, it was. So, so right. I don't know how we made it to December."

"Six of the longest months of my entire life."

"Mine, too. I remember the time, two weeks before the wedding, when I came off the ferry and you literally picked me up and carried me to the truck and didn't say a single word to me until I was under you in that little bed at the marina. We almost gave in that day."

He shuddered forty years later, thinking about the overpowering desire they'd felt for each other from the beginning. "*So* close. I was dying for you by then."

"Remind me why we decided to wait?"

"Because it was going to be your first time. I wanted it to be special—and because you were afraid I would break you."

Linda laughed at the memory. "I still worry about that sometimes." She squirmed on his lap, intentionally this time. "You're... formidable."

"You were more than up for the job."

"Very funny, but I was totally terrified that I wouldn't be able to do it, and after all that build-up, it would be a total bust."

"But it wasn't, was it?"

"Good God, no. It was spectacular."

"Mmm," he said, nuzzling her neck. "Refresh my memory. Tell me about that day."

"You haven't forgotten one minute of it."

"Tell me anyway."

Sighing with pleasure at the memory of their wedding day, she said, "It was snowing, like today, and my parents were worried that people wouldn't be able to get there. I didn't care if anyone was there, as long as you were."

"I wouldn't have missed it for anything. One of the roughest rides I've ever had on a ferry was the day before our wedding."

"Yes! You were still gray around the edges when you got to my house."

"Closest I ever came to getting sick. I thought we were going to roll over for sure. They warned us it was going to be a rough one, but no way was I missing that boat. Not after losing my mind over you for six long months."

"I was so happy to see you. I felt like we'd survived some sort of epic challenge by then."

"We had."

"We were awfully silly and dramatic, when you think about it now."

"We were crazy in love. Nothing silly or dramatic about that."

"Anyway, we had the rehearsal dinner that night at your parents' house and then the wedding the next morning. I was so nervous and excited and…"

"And what?"

"Overjoyed. I'd never wanted anything in my short life more than I wanted to be married to you."

"Forty years later, and I still love to hear you say that."

"It's still as true today as it was the day we said 'I do.'"

"For me, too." He kissed her softly and gazed into those spectacular eyes that had captivated him the first day he saw her and every day since.

"The wedding is a blur to me," she said. "I remember bits and pieces of it, walking into the church on the arm of my dad and seeing you standing there with Frankie and Kev, waiting for me. You were so handsome. My friends were all jealous that I'd landed such a stud."

"A stud," he said with a bark of laughter. "Right."

"You were—and *are*—a stud, compared to their husbands."

"Why, thank you, honey. And you are as sexy and gorgeous as you were the day I married you."

"Sure I am," she said, patting his head indulgently. "Five children later, my red bikini days are far behind me."

"You could rock that bikini today the same way you did then."

"No, I couldn't," she said, laughing. "And before you ask, I'm not putting it on for you."

He bit down on her earlobe. "I could get you to do it."

"Yes, you probably could, but it would be terribly disappointing compared to the first time I wore it for you."

"Never. Now tell me the rest of our wedding story. You're just getting to the good part."

"The 'I dos' weren't the good part?"

"Nope. That was the *legal* part. The *good* part came later."

"It certainly did."

*

After a lovely reception in a ballroom at the Biltmore Hotel, Mac's parents had surprised them with a room in the hotel for their wedding night.

"We actually get to *stay* here?" Linda had whispered to him after his parents gave him their generous gift.

"You bet we do." He pushed the button for the sixth floor and then held out his arms to her. "Most beautiful bride I've ever seen."

"I'm the only bride you've ever seen."

"That's not true. I've been to a few weddings in my time, and none of the brides were anywhere near as sexy as mine is. In fact, a few of them were downright horse-faced."

"Stop it," she said, laughing. "They were not."

"Compared to you, everyone is."

"You've already got a ring on my finger. You can probably dial the charm down a notch now."

"I've got to make sure you don't leave me when you get a better offer. I'll never dial it down."

"And I'll never get a better offer." She laid her hands flat on his chest, like she had that first day on the island, and looked up at him. "Did I mention how hot you look in a tux? My bridesmaids were drooling over you and Frank today."

"Let them drool." He wrapped his arms around her. "I got the girl. My girl. The only one I'll ever want."

"*Ever* is a really long time."

"Counting on it, babe." The elevator deposited them on the sixth floor, and Mac used the key his mother had given him to open the door. "Wait," he said when she would've proceeded into the room. "Traditions must be followed tonight, Mrs. McCarthy."

"Mrs. McCarthy," she said with a sigh. "I have to be dreaming."

"You're wide awake, and I plan to keep you that way all night long."

"All night?"

"After waiting six months, *all night*."

"Thanks for the warning."

He lifted her into his arms and carried her across the threshold into a modest but lovely hotel room, the focal point of which was a massive king-size bed. The hotel door clicked shut behind them, echoing loudly in the room.

They were *finally* alone. They were *finally* married. They *finally* had forever to spend together, and Linda was breathless with anticipation for every minute she would get to spend with him. It had been just over six months since the first time she'd laid eyes on him, but it seemed like they'd been waiting forever for this moment.

He started at her with those sexy blue eyes that made her melt from the inside. "Mac?"

"Hmm?"

"Do you feel like our parents are going to show up any second and tell us we're not really allowed to be in this room by ourselves?"

"Yeah, kinda," he said with a smile that did even crazier things to her insides than his eyes did. He was so gorgeous and all hers. "But they're not gonna show up, and we're most definitely and legally allowed to be here alone." Raising her left hand to his lips, he kissed the simple gold band he'd put on her finger earlier in the day. "Someday I'll give you a proper engagement ring, too."

"I don't need that."

"You're getting it anyway."

"If you say so."

"I do, and I'm the husband, so I'm in charge."

She raised an eyebrow to challenge that outrageous statement. "Is that how you think it's going to be?"

"Nah, I already know who the boss of this family will be."

"You're damned right about that, and don't you forget it."

"Order me to make love to my wife, will you please?"

"Mac, make love to your wife right now."

"There's nothing I'd rather do. Not one thing in this entire world."

"Me either."

"How do I get you out of this lovely dress?"

"There's a zipper under all those buttons on the back."

"Oh, thank God. I thought I'd have to undo them. I've been worried about that since our first dance when I felt how many there were."

"Would I do that to you?"

"I really hope you'll never be that cruel to me." After releasing the hook at her neckline, he drew the zipper down slowly, seeming to draw out the moment.

She trembled with anticipation and desire and a tiny bit of fear. He was so much bigger than her.

"Why did you just get tense?"

"Did I?"

"Uh-huh."

"I'm... I'm nervous."

He turned her to face him. "Why?"

"What if I'm no good at this?"

"Linda," he said, smiling. "You'll be perfect because you're perfect for me. I can't begin to tell you how much I love you. No matter what happens, it'll be special because it's you and me."

"I'm glad that at least one of us has done this before."

"And I wish I'd waited for you, but I don't believe in having regrets. Our life together officially began today, and it's going to be great. How can it not be when I've gone freaking crazy wanting you for months now?"

"I want to be what you need."

"You already are. You're everything I need and so much more than I ever expected to find." As he spoke, he moved his hands across her shoulders to remove her dress, which fell into a cloud of silk at her feet. He held her hand while she stepped out of it, and then he bent to retrieve the dress, laying it over a chair.

He did a double take when he saw the sexy corset she'd worn under her wedding dress. It did spectacular things for her breasts and cinched in her waist, accentuating the flare of her hips. His gaze traveled down to the garter belt and silk stockings.

"Holy shit," he whispered. "Are you trying to give me a heart attack?"

Giggling at his reaction, she reached up to remove his tuxedo jacket. Next, she went to work on his wraparound bow tie and then turned her attention to the studs on his shirt.

Though he wanted to rip off his own clothes and get down to business, he forced himself to remain still, to let her undress him for the first time. He took advantage of the brief pause to calm down, to remember to go slow with her, to make her first time special.

The last few months had been pure torture as they tried to hold off until today. They'd done almost everything else, driving each other crazy during long, hot nights in his little bed at the marina. This would be the first time they slept in a bed intended for two people. He doubted they'd make use of the extra space.

With all the studs removed, she dropped them onto the bedside table and set her sights on the cufflinks at his wrists.

"These are gorgeous," she said of the silver cufflinks.

"My grandfather's."

She placed them carefully on the bedside table and then helped him to remove his tuxedo shirt and the T-shirt he'd worn under it. "I hate to take this suit off you," she said. "I never want to forget how you looked in it. My sexy marina owner cleans up quite nicely."

"Glad you thought so."

"Every woman there thought so."

"I don't care what they thought. I only care what *you* thought."

She nuzzled his chest, and he got impossibly harder.

"How do I get you out of this amazing getup?"

Turning, she revealed the series of hooks and eyes that went down her back.

"How'd you get it on?" he asked as he began to undo the hooks.

"Joann did it for me. We laughed the whole time, imagining your reaction."

"I hope my reaction was satisfactory."

She giggled again. "It was very satisfactory. And you should know that Joann was insanely jealous that we were getting married first when she and Frank have been together for years."

"They're waiting until after he finishes law school."

"I wonder if they'll make it. They're so crazy for each other."

"Mmm," he said, kissing the back of her neck. "Always have been. I'm just glad we didn't have to wait years. I never would've made it."

"Me either."

He removed the last of the hooks, and the corset fell to the floor. With his arms around her, he held her close to him, feeling the tremble that traveled through her body. He cupped her breasts, loving the way her nipples tightened under his palms and the way she responded to him. She was his perfect match in every way.

"Can't wait anymore, honey," he whispered gruffly in her ear.

"Mac."

"Yeah?"

"You'll be careful with me, right?"

"God, yes, sweetheart. I'll always be careful with you."

"You're so much bigger than me. I'm afraid you'll break me."

He laughed softly. "Never. I love you too much to break you. And besides, I might be bigger than you physically, but you're way bigger than me in many other ways."

"Such as?"

"Your large personality, for one. I feel a little sorry for our future children who'll have to answer to you."

"I believe there was a compliment in there somewhere."

"Definitely a compliment. You're going to be a wonderful mother, but you aren't going to put up with any crap."

"No, I'm not."

"Does that include me, too?"

"Of course it does."

"See what I mean?"

She was laughing when he laid her down on the bed so he could help her out of the garter belt and stockings. And then she was down to just the white lacy panties that covered the one part of her he hadn't actually seen yet. He came down on top of her, gazing at her gorgeous face for a long moment before he kissed her. "I can't believe we're married and we can do this anytime we want to now. How will I work or do anything else when I have you in my bed?"

"You have to work. We both do." She'd vowed to be his partner in every way, including helping with the marina in any way she could.

He kissed a path to her breasts, feasting on one nipple and then the other.

She arched under him, her legs curling around his hips and her fingers gripping handfuls of his hair.

Mac wanted her relaxed and ready for the next step, so he focused on giving her as much pleasure as he possibly could, kissing his way to the part of her still covered in lacy white silk.

"Uh, Mac...what're you doing?"

"Relax, honey." He removed her panties and let them fall to the floor next to where he knelt. "I promise you'll love it."

"I... um... *oh*... oh God. *Mac!*" She practically tore the hair from his head, which was more than worth the sacrifice. He'd been dying to do this to her since the first night he spent with her, and now he wanted to do it every day. He wanted her to love it, so he took his time, using his tongue and fingers to arouse and prepare her for what was next. A sharp intake of breath and a keening cry preceded her climax. God, he couldn't wait to be inside her when that happened.

He brought her down slowly, continuing to stroke her with his tongue until the trembling stopped. Before she could slip out of the blissful state, he dropped his pants and boxers. He was reaching for a condom when she stopped him.

"Just you, Mac."

"We said we were going to wait to start a family."

"It won't happen right away."

"What if it does?"

"Please?"

God, if she ever knew that she could have anything she wanted when she looked at him that way, he'd be in bigger trouble than he was in already with her. They were too young and unsettled for a baby, but the thought of making love to her without protection was too tempting to resist. He was all done resisting her.

"Don't break me, okay?"

"Sweetheart," he said, kissing her as he pressed against her, easing his way in slowly. "I would never break you. It's apt to hurt a little at first, but it'll get better. I promise it'll be so good. Trust me?"

"I do. I trust you." Despite what she said, her small body shook with nerves that couldn't be overcome with words alone. He had to show her. Taking care to go slowly and to think only of her rather than the raging desire that possessed him, he gave her a little more, watching for signs of distress.

But all he saw was a tiny wince of pain that was quickly eclipsed by pleasure. Retreating, he gave her a moment to catch her breath before giving her more than she'd had before. Her back arched, and her fingers dug into his shoulders.

"Talk to me," he whispered, trying to hang on to his sanity as her internal muscles hugged him tightly. "Tell me how it feels."

"Tight."

"Mmm, so tight. So hot and wet and perfect."

"Mac."

"What, honey?"

"I want… Is there more?"

"Uh-huh. We're only halfway there."

"Oh my God."

Chuckling at her words and the expression of wonder on her face, he pushed in to the hilt. She cried out, so he froze, afraid to hurt her, to scare her, to make her not want this as badly as he did. "Talk to me, Lin."

"I-I don't have the words."

"That's good, right?"

"So good. So full and tight and hard and—"

He groaned when her innocent words made him harder than he already was. "See what happens when you talk dirty to me, honey?"

"What did I say that was dirty?"

"Full." He kissed her, biting gently on her bottom lip. "Tight." Kissing her again, he teased her tongue with his, loving the way her arms came around his neck to keep him close. "Hard," he whispered against her lips. "What do you think of this?" Withdrawing almost completely, he surged back into her.

"You need to do it again so I can say for sure."

Smiling, he did it again, harder this time, and she moaned. "Baby, I'm so close. Tell me you're close, too."

"Yes, *yes*."

Mac propped himself up on one arm and used his free hand to coax her to another orgasm that finished him off, too. As he found his own release, he knew a moment of pure panic at the thought of making her pregnant before they were ready to add to their family. But even that thought couldn't stop him from finishing what they'd started so many months ago in the sweltering-hot room in the marina—and what he'd dreamed about every night since then.

She kept her arms around him when he collapsed on top of her, throbbing with aftershocks, his heart beating harder than it ever had before. "Talk to me."

"Hi."

His lips curved into a smile against her neck. "How's it going?"

"It's going great so far. How's it going for you?"

"Best day and night of my life—and it just got a whole lot better than it already was. But only if it was good for you, too."

"It was so good. I'm glad we waited, and I'm glad I waited for you."

He wished he could say the same, but he didn't have regrets about the life he'd led before he met her. His real life began that day at Frank's when she walked onto the porch and turned his whole world upside down. After the magic they'd found together in this hotel room, he hoped his world would never be right-side up again. "I love you, honey."

"I love you, too. How soon can we do it again?"

CHAPTER 7

Big Mac laughed softly at the memory of how eager she'd been once they got the first time out of the way.

"What's so funny?" she asked from her perch on his lap.

"You were. 'How soon can we do it again?'"

She groaned. "You never let me forget that."

"How could I? I had no idea I was marrying such a wild woman."

"Stop it. I wasn't a wild woman until I married you."

"Here I thought I was getting such a sweet, innocent girl. What a shock."

Linda laughed. "Whatever you say."

"Remember how we added a second night to our stay at the Biltmore because we weren't ready to go back to reality?"

"Our little honeymoon."

"Speaking of the honeymoon we never really got to have, there's something on my desk that you need to see."

"What something?"

"You'll have to go get it and find out."

As expected, she sprang from his lap and headed for the study, where he'd left the other gift he'd spent months arranging, making sure it was perfect before he presented it to her. She returned carrying the box he'd wrapped himself in silver paper with a big silver bow on top.

"We said no gifts, and you've gone all out," she said.

He held out his arms, inviting her to return to her perch on his lap. "This one is for both of us."

As she removed the bow, he again noted a slight tremble in her hand that always meant she was excited about something. She opened the lid on the box and pushed aside the tissue paper to find a packet of papers that he'd carefully arranged. Glancing warily at him first, she returned her attention to the papers, gasping when she saw the itinerary for a trip to Paris and London—first class all the way. Nothing but the best for his bride.

"Mac," she said on a whisper, tears rolling down her cheeks.

She had always wanted to go to Paris, but they hadn't gotten there yet. In April, they would finally take the trip they'd talked about for years.

"Good surprise?" he asked.

"The best." Wiping away tears, she carefully read every page of the itinerary that would take them first to Provence for a week and then to Paris for a second week. They would travel through the Chunnel for another week in London before heading home from there. "Three whole weeks. This is incredible, Mac."

"I've heard April in Paris is the best time of year."

"That's what people say." She hugged him tightly, her tears wetting his cheek. Nothing made him happier than making her happy.

"You spoil me rotten."

"You spoiled me rotten when you gave up all your plans to come out here to live with me."

"Nothing I had planned could compare to being here with you."

"So you say, but you could've had any life—"

She kissed him before he could continue an "argument" they'd had many times. "The only life I wanted was the one I've had here with you and our family. I don't know what you think I would've ended up doing that would've been better than this."

"I've never stopped being thankful that you chose this life."

"As if you gave me any choice," she said. "You were rather relentless in your pursuit of me."

"I was, wasn't I?" he asked with a cocky grin. "But the choice was always yours, love. I would've sold the marina in a New York minute if you hadn't wanted to be here. I hope you know that."

"I do know, and I always wanted to be here as much as you did. Even that first winter when we slept in that tiny bed at the marina, freezing our butts off half the time."

He nuzzled her cheek. "Making love the other half of the time."

"I think it was more than half the time the first few years."

Laughing, he said, "You may be right about that."

"Since Mac and Maddie lost Connor, I've thought a lot about the baby we lost."

"I have, too."

"You ever wonder what he or she might've been like?"

"All the time. I figure since we had four boys before we got our girl, the baby was probably a boy."

"He'd be thirty-eight now, maybe married with a family of his own. Hard to believe it's been that long. Sometimes it feels like yesterday."

"I know. When I went to sit with Mac at the hospital this summer after they lost Connor, we talked about it a little, and I said that sometimes things happen the way they're meant to. As much as we mourned the one we lost, if he had lived, we wouldn't have had Mac when we did, and life without him…"

"Is unimaginable."

"Exactly."

"I'm very thankful for the five we have as well as Mallory, who has been such a blessing since she came into our lives," she said. "Taking a leave of absence from her job to help when Lisa Chandler was dying was such a lovely thing to do."

"Yes, it was."

"We have much to be thankful for today."

"So much." He stood, lifting her into his arms, earning a squeak of surprise from his lovely wife.

"What're you doing? You'll be crippled!"

"Stop it." He headed for the stairs. "You're light as a feather, and I've been hauling you around for forty years. Why would I quit now?"

"Um, maybe because you're sixty years old?"

"Bite your tongue, woman. Sixty is the new forty. I'm just hitting my prime."

"God help me. Where exactly are you taking me?"

"All this talk of wedding nights and making love more than half the time has put ideas in my head."

"You already had that idea today."

"Remember when I used to have it four times a day?"

"I can't say that I do. It's all a blur."

"Sure, it is," he said, chuckling as he set her on the bed and came down on top of her. "How about I refresh your memory?"

"Give it your best shot."

"Oh, I *love* when you talk dirty to me."

As she laughed, he kissed her, loving everything about her and the amazing life they'd had together.

*

Balancing his brother Adam's huge flat-screen TV in his arms while he navigated the snowy steps to the Sand & Surf Hotel, Grant McCarthy prepared for imminent disaster. Adam's frantic call that morning had woken Grant from a sound sleep to tend to his brother's instructions for last-minute party preparation.

Something had taken Adam and Abby off-island yesterday. They weren't due back until later today, which was why Adam needed Grant to deliver the TV to the hotel. Then they'd be ready to show the video Adam had made for their parents' anniversary party.

"Doesn't the hotel have a TV we could use?" Grant had asked.

"Needs to be high-def," Adam had said. "Take the one from my living room and get it over there, will you?"

Which was why Grant was currently fighting the elements to do his brother's bidding. The things he did for this family. Grant struggled to get the door open while trying not to drop the TV that had to be worth thousands, knowing Adam, who had the best of everything when it came to gadgets and electronics.

The hotel door flew open, and Grant nearly toppled into the lobby. Somehow he managed to hold on to the TV.

His cousin Laura, hugely pregnant with twins, laughed at him. "Nice save, cuz."

"Gee, thanks. Freaking Adam has me out in a blizzard doing his errands for him. Where do you want this?"

"In the restaurant. Stephanie has a plan for it."

"Of course she does." His lovely wife always had a plan, and he'd learned to go along with her plans because they led to nice things for him, too. Such as last night, when she'd planned a cozy dinner for two that had led to a nearly sleepless night. He adored her plans.

Grant carried the TV into the main dining room of Stephanie's Bistro, where the party for his parents would take place later. Stephanie was supervising her staff as they made final preparations.

"Hey, babe, where do you want the TV?"

"Oh, Grant, there you are. Over here." She directed him to a corner of the big room that had been set up for audiovisual. Adam's handiwork was all over that.

He set the TV down and then shook the blood back into his arms.

"Is that the TV from Adam's house?" Stephanie asked.

"Yep. I followed his orders to the letter."

"Still no word on why they had to go to Providence so suddenly?"

"Not that I've heard. I'm sure they'll tell us later." He kissed her nose and then her lips. "You were gone when I woke up."

"Stuff to do."

"You have to be tired after last night," he said with a private smile that she returned.

Waggling her brows at him, she said, "I'm energized."

Despite the employees working in the room, Grant put his arms around her and drew her in tight against him. The employees were used to occasional PDA from them by now.

"Please, oh, please, don't make me go to LA by myself." He was due to leave right after the New Year to meet with the production team that would make the film he'd written about her life story.

"You won't be by yourself. You've got a million meetings and things to do. I'd only be in the way."

"No, you wouldn't. I want you to be part of this, Steph."

"I've already been a part of it. I lived it. Once was enough for me."

It broke his heart to hear her say that when he was thrilled about the lucrative deal he'd struck with one of the top production companies in Hollywood. He'd gotten his dream team for the screenplay that had become a passion project to him over the last year. He wanted to take this journey with her by his side, but she showed almost no interest in being part of it, which left him with a huge dilemma.

Did he leave his new wife for what could be a month or more to tend to business, or did he step aside now that the screenplay had been sold to a company he trusted to do right by the story? The thought of removing himself from the production made him feel twitchy and nervous, but the thought of being without Stephanie for the weeks he'd need to be in LA made him feel worse.

Nothing ever went as planned in the movie business, so who even knew how long he'd have to be there?

Grant released a long, deep sigh.

"I'm sorry," she said quietly, making sure that only he could hear her. "I know how much this means to you, but I just… I can't do it, Grant. I can't relive it over and over again for the next year or however long it takes to make the movie. Just reading the screenplay was almost too much for me—and that's a huge compliment. It's brilliant and I love it. But—"

"I know, honey." Listening to her and hearing her, really hearing what she was saying, removed all thoughts of a dilemma from his mind. "I'm going to step aside as a producer."

She drew back to look up at him. "Wait. You're going to do *what?*"

"I can still be involved without being there—"

"No! You have to be there."

"Not without you."

"Grant, you're talking crazy. This movie is your baby. You have to be there to make sure it gets done right."

"I trust the team we have in place, or I wouldn't have signed with them."

"I'll go. I'll go to LA with you, and we'll figure something out for the restaurant and… I'll go."

"But you don't want to."

"It's not that."

Taking her by the hand, he led her out of the fray in the dining room, through the kitchen to her small office, shutting the door behind them. Turning to her, he propped himself on the corner of the desk and drew her in close to him. "Tell me."

"It's silly."

"No, it's not."

"No, it really is." She hesitated and seemed to force herself to meet his gaze. "You know I'm excited for you about the movie and all the interest in the story, right?"

"I think so."

"I am. I'm so proud of you and the amazing job you did with the screenplay. Charlie and I both are," she said of her stepfather.

Though he loved to hear her say that, he couldn't get past the fact that something was obviously weighing on her. "Then what is it?"

"I'm *so* happy now. The years of Charlie being in prison and me trying desperately to get him out seem like a bad nightmare that happened to someone else. Our lives have changed so much since you and Dan came along and fixed everything for us. The thought of reliving it…" She placed her hand over her belly. "It makes me feel sick, Grant."

"Come here." He put his arms around her and tucked her into the nook below his chin, where she fit like the other half of him. "I understand how you feel, because I've had the pleasure of watching you blossom since all that terrible stress was removed from your life. The last thing I want is to see you regress back to that. I promise if you come to LA with me, I'll keep you far away from what's happening with the film."

"And what kind of wife does that make me, when you can't talk about your work with me?"

"The best kind of wife, because I can talk about everything else with you. After Evan's wedding, I want to spend the rest of the winter in Southern California with you. I want you to see my place at the beach and work on your tan and shop in Beverly Hills."

She snorted with laughter. "As if I'd even know how to shop in Beverly Hills."

"You're married to a very successful screenwriter," he said with a smirk. "It's probably time you figured that out. By the time the spring rolls around, I should have all my ducks in a row for the film, and we can come back here to open the restaurant for the season. And we'll probably see Dan and Kara out there, too. He told me yesterday that snow doesn't look good on him."

Stephanie laughed. "I can hear him saying that."

"We'll have fun. I promise."

She looped her arms around his neck and kissed him. "It's always fun when I'm with you."

"I'll protect you from the past, Steph. I'll always protect you."

"The last time you took a woman with you to LA, it didn't work out so well."

"That's because Abby and I weren't meant to be, and because I had a lot to learn about what it takes to make a relationship work. I won't make those mistakes again, not when there's so much at stake." He framed her face with his hands and kissed her. "And not when there's nothing else I'd rather do than be with you."

"So I guess we're going to LA for the winter."

"Are you sure, babe? I meant it when I said I'd turn the project over to someone else."

"I'm sure. It needs to be you. You're the only one I trust completely to make sure the story gets told the right way."

"I've never told a more important story, and I probably never will again. I want the whole world to know what you did for Charlie, how you fought so tirelessly for justice."

"And I want the whole world to know how you—and Dan—finally got justice for both of us."

"Best phone call I ever made," Grant said, smiling.

"Years and years of struggle and a small fortune spent on lawyers, and all it took was one phone call from you to Dan to change both our lives. I'll never stop being grateful to both of you for what Charlie and I have now. He's so happy with

Sarah, and me... Well, I get the rest of my life with you. If there's anything better than that, I haven't found it yet."

"Me either, sweetheart."

CHAPTER 8

His ringing cell phone had Joe Cantrell reaching for the coffee table where he'd left it during a workout in the baby gym with his son, P.J. Watching those chubby arms and legs swatting at the toys above him was about the most entertaining thing Joe had ever seen.

"What's up?" he asked Seamus O'Grady, his second-in-command at the Gansett Island Ferry Company—and his mother's husband. Since Seamus was only two years older than Joe, he preferred to think of the irreverent Irishman as his mother's husband rather than his stepfather.

"I assume you've taken a glance outside today."

"Yeah, I've been keeping an eye on it."

"The last boat reported five-foot seas. I'm thinking we need to call off the rest of the day."

Joe groaned because that would strand his brothers-in-law Adam and Evan, who were due home later in the day with their fiancées, Abby and Grace, for the anniversary party, a thought he shared with Seamus.

"Planes are still flying, so the boys should be able to get home for the festivities."

"That's good news. I'll give them a heads-up. Go ahead and make the call."

"Good old Mother Nature. The one thing we can't predict with any certainty."

"No kidding. How are things at home?"

"Pretty good. The boys are excited about Christmas, and we're all looking forward to getting the addition finished. I can't believe what Mac, Shane and the rest of our friends managed to pull off in just a few months. It's a miracle, for sure."

"Everyone wants to see the boys settled and comfortable in their new home."

"No one more so than me and your mum. She's been so great with them."

"As have you."

"Ah, thanks, but I'm fumbling my way through, whereas she's a seasoned professional."

"She's a damned good mom. I can attest to how lucky Kyle and Jackson are to have her in their lives, but they're lucky to have you, too."

"With every waking day, I discover I'm the lucky one. It's nice to see them bouncing back some from the terrible loss of their poor mum. I'm starting to think they might be okay."

"They will be. I remember vividly the day my dad died, but I don't remember a lot about the immediate aftermath other than moving to the island. When I look back at those years, I remember a happy childhood even though someone was missing. That's what they'll remember, too."

"I certainly hope so. Well, I guess I'll see you tonight at the party."

"See you there. Enjoy the day off."

"I plan to."

They ended their call, and Joe fired off texts to Adam, Evan and Slim, hoping the McCarthy brothers could connect with Slim, their pilot friend, to get them to the island for their parents' party. After the texts went through, Joe did a double take when he saw the time on his phone. One o'clock and no sign of Janey yet.

"Mommy is sleeping late again, buddy." Joe picked up P.J. to bring him upstairs to check on Janey. He stepped into the master bedroom, where his wife slept, rolled up in a ball in the middle of their king-size bed, her hand tucked beneath her chin.

At the sight of his mother, P.J. let out a loud screech that jolted Janey out of a sound sleep.

Joe winced. "Sorry, honey. We were only checking on you. Didn't mean to wake you."

She sat up and reached for the baby, her hair messy around her face, which was flushed from hours of sleep. As always, Joe thought she was adorable, even if he was concerned about how much she'd been sleeping lately. No matter how early they went to bed, she couldn't seem to get enough sleep.

He sat on the edge of the bed. "You okay, babe?"

"Of course I am."

"You're sleeping a lot. You sure you're not coming down with something?"

"I feel fine." She yawned hugely. "Sorry to check out on you guys today."

"We kept ourselves busy. We had a big breakfast of applesauce and cereal and then an aggressive workout at the baby gym."

Janey smiled at the baby and then at him.

As her gaze met his, Joe noticed that her cheeks seemed fuller than usual, and an uneasy feeling gripped him. "Janey."

She guided P.J. to her breast, which also seemed bigger than usual. When had that happened?

His heart sank, and crippling fear stole the breath from his lungs.

"What?" she asked.

"Are you... Is it possible... No. You can't be. We said we weren't doing that again. It's not safe."

"Joseph, you're babbling. What the heck are you talking about?"

"You're pregnant."

Her eyes bugged. "*What?* No, I'm not."

"Yes, you are. Just like last time. All you do is sleep, and your face is rounder, and your boobs... Janey, you *are*." His chest tightened, making him feel like he was having a heart attack or an anxiety attack or possibly both at the same time, and who could blame him after the nightmare that had unfolded on the day of P.J.'s birth? He'd almost lost them both, and the thought of going through that again...

"I'm not pregnant. I'd know if I was."

"Like you did last time? I figured it out before you did then, too."

All at once, she looked stricken by the idea that she could be pregnant again. "We've been careful."

"Not as careful as we should've been a few times."

"But..." Her big blue eyes shone with unshed tears. "Joe. We can't."

Sensing she was on the verge of full-blown panic, he gathered her up without disturbing P.J., who'd dozed off at his mother's breast.

"I'm scared," she said softly.

"Me, too."

"How could this have happened *twice* without us planning it? We're not exactly stupid teenagers."

Despite his own anxiety, he smiled as he mopped up her tears. "Maybe not, but apparently we are super-fertile."

"Joe, we can't. We can't do this again." The hysteria in her voice alarmed P.J., who startled and began to cry along with his mother. "Oh God, I'm scaring him. I'm so sorry. I'm a terrible mother."

"You are not a terrible mother. You're an amazing mother."

She hiccupped on a sob. "I'm so scared, Joe."

"So am I, but before we totally freak out, we need to confirm you're actually pregnant."

"I am! I can't stay awake, my boobs hurt *and* my clothes don't fit. How did this *happen*?"

Despite the soul-deep fear he felt at the possibility of her being pregnant, his lips curved into a smile at that question. "I suspect it might've happened one of the many times you seduced me into servicing you in the last couple of months."

"I seduced *you*?" She wiped her face with the sleeve of her T-shirt. "When exactly did that happen?"

Crawling up the bed to lie next to her, Joe said, "Every time you nursed P.J. and sang lullabies to him. Every time you bathed him and giggled at the way he splashed you until you were wetter than he was. Every time you jumped out of bed when he made the littlest sound. When you walked around the house with him attached to you in that scarf thing and then when you danced until he laughed. You seduce me when you fall into bed, dead on your feet but glowing with joy after the day you've spent with our son."

Tears rolled down her cheeks, and her lips quivered. "That's the sweetest thing you've ever said."

"Then why're you crying again?"

"Because! I'm pregnant, so everything makes me cry, especially when you're sweet to me, so cut that out." She snuggled P.J. into the crook of her neck, rocking him so naturally that Joe wondered if she realized she was doing it. "Are you scared?"

"Terrified. But that's not all I am. I'm also a little excited at the thought of another P.J." He was trying not to think about the nine terrifying months that would precede the arrival of the new baby. "What're you thinking?"

"I have no idea. Mostly I'm shocked that this could've happened *again* without me knowing it. Let me tell you this, mister—if we *are* pregnant, after this, you're getting that thing snipped."

"That *thing*? Did you just refer to the part of me you love best as a *thing*?" Despite the insult to his manhood, he was relieved that she'd stopped sobbing.

"That's not the part of you I love best."

"That's not what you said the other night when you were all like, '*More*, Joe, give me *more*.'"

Her face turned bright red. "I never said that."

"Do I need to start recording these encounters?"

"If you do, I'll kill you."

"You won't kill me. You like my *thing* too much to kill me."

"I'm mad at your thing right now. He and I are in a huge fight."

Snorting with laughter, Joe said, "It's not his fault that your eggs are so *welcoming*."

She let out a low moan. "*Joe*. How can we be joking about this after what happened when P.J. was born?"

He took hold of her hand, linking their fingers and gazing into big blue eyes gone liquid with emotion and fear. "Because we're not thinking about that day right now. We're thinking about the possibility of another miracle like P.J., and we'll stay focused on that until after the holidays, when we can go see specialists on the mainland who'll tell us exactly what we're going to do to make sure that doesn't happen again."

Nodding, she said, "Yes, that's what we're going to do. And then you're getting that *thing* snipped."

Laughing, Joe gathered her into his embrace, vowing to do whatever it took to ensure that everything would be different this time. He would do anything in his power to keep her—and their baby—safe from harm.

*

"Is she down for the count?" Mac asked when Maddie came into their bedroom later that afternoon.

"Out like a light."

"Thank God for naptime."

She stretched out on the bed, where he'd been reading while she put Hailey down for a nap. Thomas had spent the previous night at Tiffany's house, and they'd see him later at the party.

"Hailey was cranky today."

"Teeth," Maddie said. "The last time we saw David, he made a comment that if any of us remembered getting teeth, we'd be traumatized for life."

"Poor baby."

"I remember going through this stage with Thomas by myself and wondering if either of us would survive it."

"It makes me sad to have missed that with him."

She turned toward him and smiled. "You won't miss much with him."

Mac put his e-reader on the bedside table and turned on his side to face her. "Whatever shall we do with a couple of hours to ourselves on a snowy afternoon?"

"Nap," she said, sighing as her eyes closed.

"That's one thing we could do."

He rested his hand on her belly, letting his fingers tease the strip of bare skin below the hem of her T-shirt.

One caramel-colored eye popped open to gauge his intentions.

"Hi there," he said with his biggest, most charming smile.

Maddie cracked up laughing. "Subtle."

"Never been my strong suit. You wanna get naked?" To his dismay, her smile faded, and her eyes went glassy with unshed tears. Propping himself up on one elbow, he asked, "Was it something I said?"

"No." She looked away, her mouth set in an unhappy frown.

"Maddie, talk to me. What's wrong?"

"If I tell you, it'll make you mad."

"Tell me anyway."

"I feel disgusting! All I do lately is puke, and I'm flabby and my boobs are huge—and how is that even *possible* when they're *huge* to begin with? One of these days, you're going to start to wonder how you ended up shackled for life to a breeding sow who stinks like sour breast milk half the time and is throwing up the other half. And if you laugh, I swear to God, Mac, I'll punch you."

"I'm not laughing." He wanted to, though. Dear God, he wanted to. "Are you for real right now? A breeding sow? What the hell, Maddie? Why would you ever think such a thing?"

"Because! Look at me! I'm a mess. My boobs are everywhere, and my belly will never be flat again, and my ass is huge and…"

He simply couldn't bear to listen to all things she thought were wrong, so he did the only thing he could think of to make it stop—he kissed her. And when she opened her mouth to protest, he took full advantage, using his tongue and teeth and every bit of love he felt for her to quiet and calm her protests.

He knew he had her when her body went limp and her arms encircled his neck to keep him close rather than push him away. Mac kissed her until he was certain he had her full attention. Then—and only then—did he break the kiss.

"I don't ever want to hear you say such things again, Madeline," he whispered against her ear. "You're talking about the woman I love more than life itself. I worship her every minute of every day, no matter what she looks like or smells like or how amazingly awesome her boobs are or how flat or not flat her belly is. My baby is in there. My other babies were in there, too. If your belly is never flat again, what the hell do I care?"

He worked her T-shirt up and over her head and unhooked her bra, releasing those spectacular breasts that were the stuff of fantasy—to him, anyway. He knew she didn't agree.

"You're always going to be hot and sexy and desirable to me." Taking hold of her hand, he laid it against his hard cock. "You feel that? That's what you do to me just walking into the room and lying down next to me. That's what happens when there's even a *possibility* that I might get to touch you and kiss you and make love to you."

Gathering her large breasts into his hands, he slid his tongue over one nipple and then the other, taking care to be gentle because she was so sensitive when she was pregnant. He loved that he knew that about her. He loved that in the second trimester, when she started to feel better, pregnancy made her super-horny.

"What're you smiling about?" she asked.

"I'm thinking about what happens in the second trimester when you spend three months basically begging me to fuck you."

"Mac! I've never said it that way."

"But you could." Looking up at her, he said, "You could say anything you wanted to me, no matter what, and I'd still love you as much as I do right now. You could gain a hundred pounds and the only thing I'd see is more of you to love."

She shook her head. "No way."

"Yes way. You don't want to talk trash about my wife, Madeline. Not to me, anyway. I love her way too much to listen to that silliness."

"It's not silly. I look totally different than I did when you first met me."

"Yes, you do. You look even better than you did then, and you looked pretty damned awesome. You know what's better?"

Eyeing him skeptically, she shook her head.

"You were too thin then because you never took the time to enjoy a meal or a glass of wine or a decadent dessert the way you can now. You were worried about everything—money, taking care of Thomas, your job, your mom. Now you're not worried about any of those things, and there's a sparkle in your eyes that wasn't there then. Three more pregnancies have made you even sexier than you were then, curvier, more lush."

"I didn't need to be curvier *or* more lush, as you put it."

"I adore your curves, and I absolutely *love* your lushness. The curvier the better, as far as I'm concerned."

"You must think I'm fishing for compliments, and I swear I'm not, even if you give really good compliments."

"I never thought that for a second. I think you're feeling a little down on yourself for some unknown reason, and you think because you're down on you I must be, too. And now that you mention it, yes, I'd love to go down on you, thank you very much."

Her sputter of laughter made him smile as he helped her out of her yoga pants and panties to make good on his statement. With her legs propped on his shoulders, he set out to show her how much he loved her. He wanted to drive her so crazy with desire that she had no time to think about all the ways he should find her lacking.

She was perfect to him in almost every way that mattered. Sure, they butted heads from time to time about silly things, such as how he drove and where he chose to leave his work clothes, but in all the most important ways they were on the same page.

Take now, for instance, when she writhed in reaction to him sucking on her clit as he drove his fingers into her.

Mac's cock throbbed with the need to get in on this, but not until he'd made her come at least once. Maybe twice for good measure. He got his wish when her first orgasm rolled right into a second one, and he worried that her cries of pleasure would wake Hailey before he finished showing her how much he loved her.

He wiped his face on his T-shirt and then whipped it up and over his head. His basketball shorts ended up around his thighs in his haste to get inside her to ride the last waves of her release.

Ah, sweet Jesus, that feels incredible. The contraction of her internal muscles nearly finished him off far too quickly.

"Look at me," he said gruffly, waiting until her gorgeous caramel-colored eyes opened to meet his gaze. "Don't ever think you're anything other than beautiful to me. Do you hear me?"

She nodded.

"This, us… it's everything. *You're* everything to me. It kills me that you think I'd ever feel anything other than crazy love for you."

Her hands coasted over his back to cup his ass, drawing him deeper into her. "Even after all this time together," she said, "sometimes I'm still surprised that you picked me."

"You crashed into me. What choice did I have but to pick you? And P.S., I'm still surprised *you* picked *me*."

"You barreled your way into my life whether I liked it or not. And P.S," she said, raising her hips to meet his thrust, "I like it. I like it a lot."

Lost in her, he said, "Mmm, me too, baby. I love you so much. You'll never know just how much."

She sighed with pleasure this time. "I think I know."

"Biggest and best thing in my life," he whispered as he kissed her again, "is my love for you and our kids. Don't ever doubt it."

After that, no words were needed.

CHAPTER 9

"I have something for you, too," Linda said to Mac as they lay in bed watching the snow fall outside. The day had grown dark early due to the thick cloud cover that had hung over the island all day.

"We said no gifts," he muttered without opening his eyes.

"And yet I have a sparkly new ring and a trip to Europe to look forward to."

"You didn't have to get me anything."

"Yes, I did, because I knew you'd go crazy the way you always do."

"I have no idea what you're talking about."

"Sure you don't. So you want your present?"

His eyes opened, and his lips curved into a smile. "Well, *yeah*."

"We have to go to Luke's."

"What?"

"You heard me, so get your lazy butt out of bed and get dressed."

"Let's grab a shower first."

"Just a shower. I can't take any more 'celebrating' today."

"Yes, you can."

"No, I really can't."

"Yes, you really can."

Their "argument" continued in the shower and as they bundled up to brave the elements. They took his truck because it had four-wheel drive—and because he would rarely be caught in her yellow Volkswagen Beetle that had been another thing he'd surprised her with a few years ago.

"So what's this present you have for me at Luke's?"

"I'm not telling you, so don't try to get it out of me." Linda couldn't wait to give him the gift Luke Harris had helped her procure after months of searching for just the right one.

"I can't believe Luke has been keeping secrets from me. I'll have to give him a piece of my mind."

"You'll do no such thing." She had called Luke to let them know they were on their way. It was hard to say who was more excited about this surprise—Linda or the young man who'd been like an extra son to them.

After a ride that took twice as long as it should have due to the snow, they pulled into Luke's driveway.

"Go on back to the barn," Linda said, referring to the building where Luke did his boat restoration work.

"Curiouser and curiouser," Mac said.

"Just hush and do what you're told."

His grunt of laughter made her smile. "You've always been such a bossy little thing."

"You've always needed to be bossed."

He placed his big hand on her thigh and squeezed. "Oh baby, boss me. Please boss me."

Rolling her eyes at him, she said, "I keep thinking one of these days you might actually grow up."

"That ain't never gonna happen."

Which was fine with her, not that she could say so to him.

Luke waited for them with the doors to the barn open. The surprise was covered with a tarp, and Linda couldn't wait to see Mac's reaction when he realized what was under the cover.

They got out of the truck and went into the garage.

Linda gave Luke a quick hug, and he shook hands with Mac.

"Happy anniversary, you guys," Luke said.

"Thank you, honey," Linda replied.

"What're you two up to?" Mac asked.

Luke looked to her. "You ready to show him?"

"So ready." They'd been working on this surprise for almost a year.

"It's under there," Luke said, gesturing to the tarp.

Mac approached the tarp like it was wired with explosives, tentatively lifting it.

"Oh, for crying out loud, Mac," Linda said. "Just pull it off, will you?"

He did as directed and gasped at the sight of the gleaming boat. "Is that a…"

"Nineteen thirty-six Chris-Craft five-five-seven," Luke said.

Mac had a smaller classic Chris-Craft runabout that he loved, but they couldn't sleep on that one.

"Holy moly," Mac said, running his hand over the shiny brightwork and creamy white paint. "What a beauty."

"It is now," Luke said with a chuckle. He'd been working on the boat for six months, ever since Linda located it rotting away in a boatyard in Wisconsin. "You've got the pictures?"

"I sure do." Linda produced an album from her purse that documented the boat's journey from broken down to fully restored.

"Wow," Mac said as he flipped through the photos. "This is incredible. What a great surprise."

"I figured we could do some cruising on this one," Linda said.

"We sure can." He hugged her tightly. "Thank you so much, Lin. And Luke, you did an amazing job, as always."

"It was fun. The best part was pulling one over on you."

Big Mac laughed. "Which is not easy to do."

"No, it isn't. Hope you guys are having a really great day. You surely deserve it after not only raising your own family but also helping out with a few special cases."

Big Mac released Linda to put both hands on the shoulders of the man who'd showed up at the marina as a fatherless fourteen-year-old looking for a job and had become one of them in the ensuing years. "You're family to us, Luke, and we wouldn't have it any other way."

Luke swallowed hard. "Thank you," he said softly. "You've both meant more to me than you'll ever know."

Big Mac hugged him, and then Linda did the same.

"We love you," she said.

"Same," Luke said.

Sensing they were about to reduce him to tears, Linda took Mac by the hand. "Luke has graciously agreed to keep the boat here for the winter."

"You can keep it here every winter. I've got plenty of room for it."

"Thanks again, you guys," Mac said, taking another long look at the boat. "I love it."

Smiling at Luke, Linda gave him a giddy thumbs-up, thrilled that their gift had been such a hit with the man who was almost impossible to surprise.

*

It was still snowing when a car service delivered Adam and Abby to the Westerly airport for the late-afternoon flight home to Gansett. Since their conversation earlier, Abby had been quiet and withdrawn. Though she'd agreed to his plan to get married on New Year's Eve, he knew their accord was fragile and could shatter at any moment.

The same could be said for Abby. He was afraid to touch her for fear that she, too, might shatter.

While Abby went to use the restroom, Slim Jackson, his pilot friend, met him with a bro hug. "Good to see you, buddy."

"You, too," Adam replied. "How's Florida treating you?"

"Oh, you know, nonstop sun and fun. It gets a little boring after a while."

"Sure, it does." Adam gestured to the snow that continued to fall. "This is so much better."

Slim laughed. "It does make things interesting."

"We're okay to fly to the island?"

"Absolutely. It's barely freezing, so we'll de-ice and go. I wouldn't want you to miss your parents' party. Hell, I don't want to miss it, either."

"Are Evan and Grace here yet?"

"They're about fifteen minutes out."

"Oh, good. When I heard the ferries were canceled, my heart sank. Months of planning and two of us might miss it?"

"I'd never let that happen."

"Today I'm thankful for old friends who know how to fly."

"Who you calling old?"

They were laughing and joking around the way they usually did when Abby joined them, giving Slim a perfunctory hug.

"Nice to see you," she said in a dull, flat tone that had Slim raising a brow in question to Adam.

He dodged the inquiry and put his arm around her.

"Good to be home," Slim said.

"Are you sticking around after the holidays?" Abby asked.

"I'm not sure yet. Depends on a few things."

Adam wanted to pursue that further because Slim always had the best stories, but the arrival of Evan and Grace a few minutes later had them all heading for Slim's Cessna Citation for the flight to the island.

Grace was worried about flying in the storm, but Slim assured her they'd be fine.

"I wouldn't do it if I wasn't sure it was okay," Slim said.

"He's the best pilot I know, baby," Evan said.

"He's the *only* pilot you know," Grace replied with a saucy grin that made Adam smile. He looked over to find Abby gazing out the window, a blank expression on her face that reignited his earlier worries.

Though she'd agreed to marry him, her heart wasn't in it, and that killed him after everything they'd been through to get to this point in their lives together. Both of them had overcome failed relationships and heartbreak to take a chance on each other, and he'd never been happier than since the magical week they'd spent together last summer.

That had been the start of everything, and their wedding needed to be a celebration of their love, not a Hail Mary play to save a relationship that hadn't needed saving before yesterday.

As they taxied to the runway for takeoff, Abby sat right next to him, her thigh touching his, but she was a million miles from him, the gulf between them so wide it was frightening. What would he do if she permanently checked out of their relationship? Adam shook off that thought as quickly has he had it.

He wouldn't let her do that. Reaching for her hand, he linked their fingers and held on tight as they hurtled down the runway, lifting off into the cloud-filled sky on the short flight home to Gansett. The thick clouds made for a bumpy climb.

Abby tightened her grip on Adam's hand. She was unnerved by the bumps and hung on to him for comfort. How sad was it that such a small thing filled him with hope?

He released her hand to put his arm around her, encouraging her to rest her head on his shoulder, which she did. "Everything's going to be okay, Abby." Adam hoped she knew he was talking about far more than the bumpy flight.

She released a deep breath and relaxed against him.

Adam ran his fingers through her long, dark hair. He loved her silky, shiny hair, and the thought of her losing it killed him. But that would never change the fact that his heart belonged to her, completely and absolutely.

In front of them, Evan and Grace giggled like high school kids on a first date. And then they were kissing like two people who'd spent most of the last month apart and were thrilled to be back together. Good for them. Adam would never begrudge his brother the happiness he deserved. He just wished that he and Abby could go back to yesterday morning, before they had real problems, before they knew the results of tests she'd had two weeks ago.

He wanted to go back in time twenty-four hours, when it would've been impossible to imagine her saying the things she'd said this morning, things that had rocked the foundation under him. How could she think for one minute that he would leave her rather than face whatever might happen to her? How could she give voice to such a thought? How were they supposed to go forward now that she'd said such things out loud?

Adam no sooner had these disturbing thoughts than he shook them off, determined to file them under things Abby said when confronted with a life-changing condition. It wasn't her talking. It was the fear. That had to be it, because any other possible explanation didn't bear consideration.

His Abby, the woman he loved with his whole heart and soul, didn't want to spend a day apart from him, let alone the rest of her life. The very idea of a life without her at the center of it left him feeling bereft. He would be, quite simply, inconsolable if she gave up on them.

Which was why he was insisting on a wedding next week. He had to get that second ring on her finger before she could do something stupid like actually break up with him. He couldn't let that happen.

"You okay, honey?" he asked, speaking close to her ear so she could hear him over the drone of the plane's engines.

She nodded.

Right next to him but still a million miles away...

Twenty minutes after they took off, Slim began the final approach to the Gansett Island airport. And as the wheels touched down on the island, Adam relaxed ever so slightly. They were home, and he could wage war—if that was what it took—to keep Abby right where she belonged—with him.

*

At six o'clock, Ned and Francine arrived at the "White House," as the locals called the McCarthy home. Big Mac's best friend was turned out in a blue sport coat, khaki pants, new boat shoes, a blue shirt and a *tie*. Ned, who preferred his clothes old and holey, had worn a *tie* for him.

"Must be one hell of an occasion," Big Mac said as he hugged his longtime best friend.

"T'aint every day yer best friends celebrate forty years a marriage," Ned said.

"I suppose that's true." Big Mac hugged and kissed Ned's wife, Francine, who glowed with happiness these days. Long gone was the bitter, spiteful woman who'd been knocked down once too many times by life before she ended up with her one true love.

"Congratulations, Mac," Francine said. "You two set the gold standard."

"What's this about gold?" Linda asked as she came into the living room, where Big Mac was fixing drinks for the four of them.

"Gold standard," Ned said. "Ya set the bar awfully high fer the rest a us."

Linda kissed his cheek and hugged him for a long moment, making him blush the way she always did when she showed him affection.

"Happy anniversary, doll," Ned said.

"Thanks, old friend."

"T'aint no one in this room is old. We're young at heart."

"That we are," Linda said, beaming with happiness. She wore a slinky, sexy black dress and sky-high heels that had made Mac want to skip the festivities to have her all to himself tonight. But he'd never do that to the kids, suspecting they'd gone to some trouble for the occasion.

Linda hugged Francine, and Big Mac was struck by how far the two women had come from the days when Linda had had no choice but to report Francine for repeatedly writing bad checks to pay her bar bill at the hotel. Linda's complaints—and those of other island merchants—had resulted in a three-month jail sentence that seemed like a lifetime ago now that Francine was happily married to Ned. Not to mention, her daughter Maddie was married to their son Mac. Speaking of happy.

The women shared two grandchildren, and had managed to put the past where it belonged for the sake of their families.

While Francine and Linda chatted about their favorite subjects—Thomas and Hailey—Big Mac took Ned aside. "I was thinking about you today."

"What about me?"

"Remember when you were practically the only person I knew on this island?"

"Sure do," Ned said with a chuckle. "Gave ya a ride over to North Harbor to check out the marina that first time."

Big Mac smiled at his old friend. "I was thinking, too, about how you sold me this house for dirt cheap."

"Ya had yer bride sleeping in the back room at the marina. Desperate times. Someone had ta do somethin'."

Throwing his head back, Big Mac let out a big laugh. He put his hand on Ned's shoulder. "Just want you to know—I never could've gotten through those first couple of years without Linda. But I couldn't have done it without you, either. Getting in your cab that day was one of the best things I ever did in my whole life."

Ned blinked furiously. "Aww, shit…yer all sappy today. Hell, yer sappy every day."

"Maybe so, but I wanted you to know, just the same."

"Means a lot ta me. Before Francine came back ta me, this was my home as much as yours. You and Linda and yer family…my family, too," he said gruffly. "Woulda been a lonely life without y'all ta keep things interesting fer me."

"This life of ours wouldn't have been the same without you, either. My third brother."

Ned continued to blink back tears, so Big Mac changed the subject before they turned into a couple of blubbering idiots.

"How big of a deal are we looking at tonight?"

Ned's eyes widened.

"Did you really think they were fooling Voodoo Mama?"

"Suppose not," Ned said with a chuckle. "Y'all will act surprised so they don't think I spilled the beans, woncha?"

"Of course. So, big deal, small deal?"

"I ain't tellin ya nothin', so quit askin'."

"We should get going," Francine said. "Our reservation is for six-thirty."

"After you, my dear." Ned followed his wife to get their coats in the foyer.

"Ready for this?" Linda asked as she took hold of Mac's outstretched hand.

"You bet. How about you?"

"It's already been an amazing day. I'm looking forward to an amazing evening with our family."

Mac held her coat. "It was a pretty great day, wasn't it?"

"The best. The ring, the trip, the memories… Doesn't get much better."

Mac couldn't agree more. It had been a fantastic day, and now he couldn't wait to see what their kids had planned for the evening.

CHAPTER 10

Dashing through the snow, the foursome made their way to the front porch of the Sand & Surf Hotel. Mac kept a tight hold on Linda's arm so she wouldn't fall on the slippery sidewalk or stairs with those crazy shoes on. They entered through the main doors of the hotel, where their family waited to greet them.

"Surprise!"

Adam, Abby, Mallory, Janey, Joe, Evan, Grace, Mac, Maddie, Stephanie, Grant, Thomas, Hailey and P.J. made up the welcoming committee.

Thomas stepped forward to present a wrist corsage made of white roses to Linda and a white rose for Big Mac's lapel. "Are you surprised, Papa?" Thomas asked.

"So surprised, pal. How did you keep this a secret?"

The blond boy smiled widely. "I promised Daddy I wouldn't tell."

Big Mac hugged the little boy who'd made him a grandfather when Mac married his mother. "You did a good job keeping the secret." Standing upright, he accepted a hug from Evan, who'd spent the last three weeks touring with Buddy.

"So good to have you home, son."

"Good to be home. Happy anniversary."

"Thank you."

After lots of hugs and kisses and congratulations, Stephanie said, "Ready to go in? We've got a table all ready."

"Ready when you are," Linda said, reaching for Big Mac's hand.

Though he was prepared for a party, he was floored by just how many people had braved the elements to come celebrate with them. The main dining room of Stephanie's Bistro was packed with friends and neighbors and extended family, who broke into a long round of applause as he and Linda entered the room.

Overwhelmed by the outpouring, his heart expanded in his chest. His brothers Frankie and Kevin hugged him, as did his adorably pregnant niece Laura, his nephews Shane, Riley and Finn, Linda's sister Joan and her family, Alex and Jenny Martinez, Dan Torrington, Kara Ballard, Luke and Sydney Harris, Paul Martinez and his fiancée Hope Russell, Shane's fiancée Katie Lawry and her brother, Laura's husband, Owen Lawry. Katie and Owen's mother Sarah and her fiancé Charlie Grandchamp were there, as were Carolina and Seamus O' Grady, Maddie's sister Tiffany and her husband Blaine Taylor, David Lawrence and his girlfriend Daisy Babson, and Jared and Lizzie James. Everyone who was anyone to them had come. Even the Mayor Upton and his wife, Verna, were there.

He saw Linda receive a tearful hug from Mallory.

Though a hundred people wanted to talk to him, he stayed with Linda, needing her close to him as much today as he had on their wedding night night forty years ago. While they visited with their guests, Stephanie's waitstaff delivered glasses of champagne that were replaced the minute they were empty. After a while, they were shown to a head table that included the members of their original wedding party, including Frank and Kevin and Linda's friends from Providence College. Frank's beloved wife Joann, who died of cancer more than twenty years ago, was the only one missing.

And then someone handed their son Mac a microphone, and everything went downhill from there in the most hilarious way possible.

"Oh, dear God," Linda muttered as Mac cleared his throat dramatically to get everyone's attention.

"As Mac and Linda's oldest and wisest son," Mac said to jeers from his brothers, "it's my pleasure to welcome you to their fortieth anniversary celebration. When I first had the idea for this party last summer," he said to more moans and groans as he spoke now directly to them, "we tried to think of how we could do justice to the example you set for us, the life you've led together, your lifelong love affair."

He made a choking sound. "That was Janey's contribution, and for the record, I voted to leave that part out."

Their guests were crippled with laughter while Mac and Linda just shook their heads at his usual irreverence. From the day he was born, Malcolm John McCarthy Junior had been a character, to say the least.

"After many conversations," Mac said, "we decided that all we really needed to do was bring together your family and closest friends. We knew that's all you'd need to be happy—because that's all you've ever needed."

Aww jeez, Big Mac thought. *He's going to make me cry in front of all these people.*

"Mom, we like to call you Voodoo Mama, because you've always been wise to whatever we were up to. I'd be shocked, in fact, if we actually managed to surprise you tonight."

Linda made a zip-her-lips-and-throw-away-the-key gesture that fooled none of her five children. They knew her far too well.

"Despite your voodoo ways, we've always known that you had our backs no matter what. We appreciate the way you've made our spouses and significant others part of our family, and we all agree that you're a world-class grandmother."

As Linda dabbed at her eyes, Mac put his arm around her.

"You're the one who makes it all happen. You made the White House a home not only to us but also to our friends and now the families we're creating. And everyone knows you're the brains behind the hotel—and the marina."

"Now wait just a minute," Big Mac said, smiling at his son.

"You can't deny it, Dad."

"I wouldn't even try."

"And you, Dad," Mac continued, "are the emotional heart of our family, the one we run to—to this day—whenever the slightest little thing goes wrong, because we know, without a shadow of a doubt, that you'll know just what to say to make us feel better. When we were kids, we used to be embarrassed by how much you loved us. Now, we're thankful."

Holy moly. Linda handed him a tissue that he gratefully accepted.

"You also taught us how to have fun, because no one—and I do mean *no one*—knows how to have fun quite like you do. Whether it's a Wiffle ball game on the dock, a bonfire on the beach, coffee-and-donut hour at the marina or a fishing trip for all the guys you love best, you bring the fun no matter where you go. One of my earliest memories is catching crabs with you on the docks, and now that'll be one of my son's earliest memories, too. Not only did you and Mom teach us how to be married, you also taught us how to live life to the fullest by showing us when to work and when to play."

Mac raised his glass of champagne. "Please join me, my sisters Janey and Mallory, and my brothers Grant, Adam and Evan, in saluting our parents on their fortieth anniversary."

After shouts of "hear, hear" and the insistent tinkle of silver on crystal as the guests called on Big Mac to kiss his bride, which he was more than happy to do, Mac directed their attention to the huge flat-screen TV at the other end of the room. "Take a look back with us, thanks to Adam's video wizardry. Enjoy."

The lights dimmed, and the TV came to life along with the song "Time of My Life." They giggled at the photos of themselves as a young couple, including one taken the day they met at Frank's house, up through their wedding.

"Hey!" Linda said. "No wonder I couldn't find my wedding album today!"

"I'll have it back to you in the morning, Mom," Adam said.

The video included photos of each of their children as babies, scenes from the early days at the marina when Linda had run the restaurant while he oversaw the docks, a picture of them holding the keys to the hotel—which they bought three years after the marina—and images of early Christmases at the White House with toddlers underfoot.

A ripple of laughter went through the room when a photo of four pajama-clad little boys precariously balancing their newborn sister appeared on the screen.

"Should've dropped her when we had the chance," Evan said.

"I could've beat you up even then," Janey said.

"She could've," Grant said.

"Children, stop bickering," Linda said. "I'm watching my video."

"Adam's going to be her favorite now," Mac said.

"He already was," Linda said, setting off a furor at the "kid table."

Summers with Laura and Shane, proud new drivers, proms, graduations, weddings and grandchildren. It had gone by far too quickly. Big Mac was particularly touched by the photo toward the end of the video of Mallory with him and Linda as well as one with her and the five siblings she hadn't known she had, both of which had been taken at Grant's wedding this past Labor Day.

The video told the story of a beautiful life from the very beginning and ended with a photo of him kissing Linda in what he'd thought was a private moment at Jenny and Alex's wedding in October. It had been captured for all the world to see and touched him more than almost anything else in the video. Their story, his story, began and ended with her.

As the video finished, the room erupted into applause. Big Mac kissed Linda, lingering longer than he normally would in public, and then leaning his forehead against hers. "What a story," he whispered.

"What a story, indeed."

"Extremely well done, Adam," he said.

"Thank you," Adam said. "It was fun."

"Mom and Dad," Mac said, "Evan was put in charge of the music for tonight, and first up is your wedding song, 'You're The First, The Last, My Everything,' by none other than Barry White. And let me apologize in advance to our guests for all the disco you'll be hearing tonight, but that was their groove way back then. Dad, how about you dance with your bride?"

Mac took Linda's hand to guide her to the dance floor in the middle of the big room. As he took her into his arms, it felt like yesterday since he'd done the same thing in a ballroom at the Biltmore. God, they'd been so young and so in love and so determined to make a life on the island.

And against many odds, they'd done it.

*

"What's wrong?" Grace nudged Abby's shoulder, which was when Abby realized she'd zoned out of the party.

"Nothing."

"Something's up. You've been super-quiet since we met at the airport. What were you guys doing on the mainland, anyway?"

"Last-minute Christmas shopping in Providence."

"Did you have a fight with Adam?"

"No."

"Abby! Come on! This is me. I know you too well. What's going on?"

To her horror and mortification, Abby's eyes filled with tears.

"Oh my God. What?"

She couldn't say it. Saying the words out loud, to someone other than Adam, who'd been with her when she first heard the news, would make it real. Her throat closed up, and the tears spilled down her cheeks.

"Abby." Grace put an arm around her. "Whatever is wrong, we can fix it."

Abby shook her head. If only it were that simple. She wiped her face with a napkin, determined not to ruin Big Mac and Linda's night by having an emotional breakdown. "Adam and I have been trying to have a baby for a long time." She wiped away more tears. "We found out this week why it's not happening. Why it may never happen. I have something called polycystic ovary syndrome."

"Oh. Oh, Abby. I'm so sorry."

"You know what it is?"

Grace nodded. "I've heard of it and read about the treatments in my journals."

"Then you know it's more than just fertility challenges."

"Yes, but I also know it can be managed."

"That's what my doctor said, too. I know there are worse things they could've diagnosed me with, but the stuff online—"

"Stay off the Internet, Abby. Trust me on that. You might read about thirty different things that can happen, but only two of them will happen to you. Do you really need to worry about *all* of them?"

Grace made a good point.

"I'm so scared, Grace. I've wanted to be a mother for as long as I can remember, and the possibility that it won't happen is devastating."

"It may not happen naturally, but there're lots of ways to become a mother that don't require you to carry a child, Abby. You know that."

"I do know, but still…"

"It's devastating to hear you might not be able to get pregnant."

Abby nodded and wiped away more tears.

"I'm sure the doctors told you there's lots they can try."

"They did."

"What did Adam say?"

"All the right things, of course. Right down to scheduling our wedding for New Year's Eve so I can't escape."

Grace stared at her, agape. "Do you *want* to escape?"

"Of course that's not what I want, but it's not fair to him to be saddled with this."

"Abby, how can you say that? He *loves* you. He's crazy about you."

"I know he is! And I love him, but he didn't sign on for this. I could go bald and get chest hair and never be able to have a baby and… Are you *laughing*?"

"I don't mean to laugh, because it's honestly not funny, but you're focused on the worst-case scenario before you even have all the information. It's very possible that none of that will happen to you, but you're willing to sacrifice the love of your life for something that *might* happen?"

"It's not what I want, but it might be what's fair."

"Can I be really blunt with you right now?"

"When are you anything but blunt?" Abby asked with a ghost of a smile.

"You've just received very upsetting news that has you understandably reeling. There're a lot of things you don't know yet and may not know for some time. The worst thing you could do while you're in crisis mode is to make major decisions that affect you and Adam. *That* wouldn't be fair to either of you."

"You're right. I know you are."

"He's been watching us the whole time we've been talking."

Abby looked over to the nearby table where Adam was sitting with Mac and Maddie. His niece, Hailey, was asleep in his arms, and sure enough, he was keeping a close eye on her while he talked to his brother. Seeing him holding the baby drew a sob from deep inside Abby. He would be the best father ever, and the thought of that not happening cut her to the quick.

Grace hugged her. "You and Adam will get through this. We'll all be there for you, and we're going to put together one hell of a New Year's Eve wedding for you guys."

"I feel like we're stepping on your toes by sneaking our wedding in ahead of yours."

"Don't be silly. Yours will be weeks before ours, and if you wanted to do it the same damned day, I wouldn't care. I get to marry Evan, and that's all that matters."

Abby rested her head on Grace's shoulder, thankful for the love and support of such a good friend who would soon be her sister-in-law, too.

CHAPTER 11

"Is Abby okay?" Mac asked Adam. "She looks like she's crying over there with Grace."

"Adam's throat tightened, making it impossible to speak. He dropped his head to press a kiss to Hailey's head, her soft hair brushing against his lips.

"Bro, what's wrong? You guys haven't been yourselves tonight."

With Maddie engaged in conversation with her sister and mother, Adam was tempted to unload on Mac. "If I tell you, you can't tell anyone else. I mean it, Mac. Top secret."

"Of course. I'm not always a mouthy buffoon."

Adam raised a brow, appreciating his brother's attempt at levity.

"Okay, most of the time I am, but I can be serious when I need to be. Talk to me."

"We've been trying to have a baby for a while now, and when it didn't work the old-fashioned way, we went to see a specialist in Providence." He cleared his throat, determined to get through this without breaking down. "Yesterday we found out she has something called polycystic ovary syndrome."

"What the hell is that?"

"Long story short—it's going to make having a baby very challenging, if not impossible, but that's the least of it. Higher risk of all sorts of diseases including cancer and diabetes, among other things."

"Damn," Mac said, exhaling. "I'm so sorry, Adam."

"The worst part isn't even the medical issue. It's that she thinks she needs to let me go so I can be with someone who can give me what I want."

"She actually *said* that?"

"Yeah."

"Shit."

"No kidding, right? As if I'd run for the hills at the first sign of trouble. I have to be honest… She really hurt me by saying that."

"I can only imagine. What did you say?"

"I told her we're getting married on New Year's Eve, and I wouldn't hear any more talk of her running away or thinking she isn't what I want and need. Does she honestly think that I wouldn't want her if she can't have kids? Like that's all she's good for? Making babies?"

Mac rested a hand on Adam's shoulder. "You have to see this from her point of view, Adam. She was freaking out and probably said things she shouldn't have. She's scared and worried that you might reject her because of this."

"I would never reject her."

"You and I know that, and she should, too, but she's reeling. You've got to give her a pass on anything she said in the last couple of days. It's coming from the panic, not from her. She loves you. We all know that."

"I thought I knew it, too, but she was so detached, I guess you could say, and she's never like that with me."

"Give her a few days to get her head around this thing, and try not to go to worst-case scenario. When she's had a chance to accept her diagnosis and recover her footing, she'll be okay."

Adam wanted to believe that Mac was right, but he had a bad feeling that things could get a whole lot worse before they got better.

*

As the evening began to wind down, Laura McCarthy Lawry worked her way through the room, handing out key cards to family members. Her gift to her aunt and uncle was having their entire family spend the night under the same roof. The hotel staff had delivered everyone's bags, including the one Janey had packed for her parents, to their rooms during the party.

"The key to the honeymoon suite," Laura said, presenting the key card to her Uncle Mac.

His low chuckle made her smile. "We're a long way from the honeymoon suite, sweetheart, but we're looking forward to the sleepover with the kids." He kissed her forehead. "Thank you for arranging it."

"My pleasure. It'll be fun to have everyone here for the night."

"We're glad no one has to drive in the snow after partying."

"That was my thought, too."

"It's a lot for you, though. Are you feeling okay?"

"I'm feeling great for someone who's bigger than a whale." She rested a hand on her hugely pregnant belly. "I'll be glad to see these two linebackers born."

"I'll bet." He put his arm around her. "I was thinking about the day I met your Aunt Linda today, which means I was also thinking about your mom. She'd be so proud of you and Shane."

Unprepared for the sweet sentiment, Laura worked through a surge of emotion. The pain of losing her mother to cancer when she was just nine could still hit at the strangest of times, even all these years later. "Thank you for saying so. That means a lot to me."

"Your old man sure is happy these days, huh?" They looked toward the dance floor, where Frank was dancing with his girlfriend, Betsy Jacobson.

"He waited a long time for Betsy to come along. I couldn't be happier for him."

"Me too. I wondered at times if he'd ever get over losing Jo. Those two were quite a pair from the very beginning. Joined at the hip."

"I actually remember that. They were always dancing in the living room, laughing, whispering, kissing."

"I'm glad you remember them that way." Big Mac gave her another squeeze and kissed the top of her head. "Life goes on even when you think it won't. Your dad is living proof of that."

"Yes, he is. And then there's Kevin."

"Ahhh, Kevin. Gotta say, didn't see that one coming."

Her uncle Kevin was wrapped up in Chelsea, the bartender from the Beachcomber, slow dancing to a fast song.

"He's crazy about her," Big Mac said.

"It looks as if the feeling is mutual."

"Yes, it does. Good for him after what happened with Deb."

Owen came up behind her and slid his arm around her waist. "You promised you wouldn't be on your feet all night, and you're on your feet."

"Oh, busted by my keeper."

"He's right," Big Mac said. "You need to be taking it easy, not inviting your entire family to sleep at the hotel."

"I hired some people to help with that," Laura said with a wink. "Don't worry."

"Thanks again for inviting us to stay and for arranging babysitters for the kids and everything else you did to make tonight special for us," Big Mac said.

"Are you kidding? You and Auntie Linda saved my childhood. There's nothing Shane and I wouldn't do for you." She went up on tiptoes to kiss his cheek and hug him. "Love you."

"Love you, too, sweetheart."

Laura let Owen lead her toward a seat next to the final person she needed to see about the key cards, her new cousin Mallory. "Just the woman I was looking for," Laura said. "Here's the key to your room for the night."

"This is so nice of you, Laura. Thank you for including me."

"Of course I included you. You're family now."

"I'm still getting used to having a big family, let alone one as awesome as this one."

"We are pretty awesome," Laura said, making Mallory laugh.

"I wish my mom had told me who my father was a long time ago."

"We do, too, but we'll make up for lost time now that we have you here with us."

"My dad is pressuring me to move out here where I belong—and those are his words, in case you wondered."

"I had no doubt," Laura said, laughing.

"I keep telling him I have a job and a house and a life in Providence, but he can be rather convincing when he sets his mind to something. And I have to admit, I'm tempted to chuck my life there and go for it. I spent forty years wondering who my father was, and now that I know him and the rest of you, I want to be here all the time."

"I don't blame you. Maybe you'll figure out a way to make that happen at some point."

"That would be nice. It was great to be here over the summer to help with Lisa Chandler's hospice care, and my job was very accommodating of the leave of absence."

"We loved having you here, and I know everyone appreciated what you and Katie and Hope did for Lisa."

"I was honored to be part of it, and I'm thrilled to see the boys doing so well with Seamus and Carolina."

"They've been so great with the boys, and so has everyone who helped to build the addition to their house."

"This island is a special place."

"It really is, and *if* you should decide to make it your home, we'll make sure you're never bored or lonely."

"You sound like my dad," Mallory said with a smile. "He says the same thing."

"We must be related. You're staying for Christmas, right?"

"Wouldn't miss my first Christmas with my new family for anything."

"Good," Laura said, smiling at her new cousin.

*

With the evening beginning to wind down, Kevin was eager to take advantage of the key card Laura had given him earlier to take Chelsea upstairs to bed. But he held off out of respect for his brother and sister-in-law, who'd want to spend time with their family after the other guests left.

When they were down to just family, Laura stepped up to the microphone. "Everyone go slip into something more comfortable and meet us in the salon for nightcaps, freshly baked chocolate chip cookies and entertainment from my gorgeous husband, Owen, and my talented cousin Evan."

"How come he gets to be the talented one?" Owen asked.

"Yeah, and why is he the gorgeous one?" Evan retorted.

Laughing at their good-natured bickering, Kevin looked down at Chelsea, who'd knocked his socks off tonight with the sexy, shimmery silver dress she'd worn to the party with three-inch heels that showed off her incredible legs. He was completely gone over her and had been for months now, ever since that memorable night in September when she'd blatantly propositioned him.

"Um, Kev?"

"Yeah?"

"What're you thinking about?"

"Why do you ask?"

She subtly rubbed against his cock, which had hardened at the thought of the first night he spent with her.

"I'm thinking about you, as usual, and that's what tends to happen when you're on my mind or in my arms or under me in bed."

Her soft moan was music to his ears. He loved the way she responded to him. One glorious night with her had made him realize how utterly lacking the last few years of his marriage had been, and now he was seriously addicted to her. He'd be the happiest guy on earth, except for one thing—her insistence on keeping their "relationship" to sex only.

He was getting to the point where the frustration of being stuck in neutral with her was starting to get to him, but he'd been reluctant to push the issue, especially when he was having the best sex of his life with her. She'd agreed to attend his family party tonight, but he'd had to do some serious begging and pleading to get her to agree to something other than sex.

"Let's go get changed." He took her by the hand and led her upstairs to the second floor. They'd been told to pack a bag to spend the night, and Kevin couldn't wait to sleep next to her for a full night. Up until now, she'd always gotten up to go home after they had sex—or expected him to leave if they were at her place.

Her arm's-length approach was starting to make him a little crazy. If he were being honest with himself, he would confess that he'd never felt about Deb the way he did Chelsea. He and Deb had been great friends and had brought up two exceptional sons together, but they'd never burned up the sheets the way he and Chelsea did.

He turned on the light to reveal a king-size bed and a renovated room done in a coastal theme.

"This is so nice," Chelsea said. "I'd wondered what the new rooms looked like."

Kevin couldn't have cared less about the decorating. Not when he had Chelsea alone in a room with a huge bed. He backed her up to the bed until her legs connected with the mattress. She fell onto the bed, bringing him down with her.

"I thought we were getting changed," she said with a sexy smile.

"We are, but in order to get changed, first we must get naked."

"You are too much, Kevin McCarthy."

"Am I?" he asked, propping himself up on his arms so he could see her face.

"No."

"You look so beautiful tonight."

"I'm glad you think so."

"Then again, you always look beautiful."

As she often did when he complimented her, she diverted her gaze. In the past, he'd let that go, unwilling to scare her off by pushing her for things she said she didn't want. But they'd been together—or whatever they were—for months now, and he was finding it harder not to push for more.

"Was it something I said?"

"No."

As he bent to kiss her neck, he sent his left hand to find the hem of her dress, drawing it up to where a thigh-high stocking connected with soft skin. She trembled madly under his touch, her legs falling open in encouragement. The mixed signals were killing him. She was always willing and responsive in bed but closed off and remote out of bed.

"Chels," he whispered.

"Hmm?"

"Can we talk?"

She raised her hips to press against his hard cock. "Right now?"

Though he was torn by the desire that pounded through him, the torment of wanting more from her than she was willing to give trumped desire for once. He dropped his head to her chest.

She ran her fingers through his hair, the loving caress giving him the hope he badly needed. "What's wrong?"

"I want to know why you won't let this be more than just sex."

Sighing, she said, "We've talked about this. You just got out of a thirty-year marriage, Kevin. You're not even officially divorced yet, and most rebound relationships end in disaster. I don't want to be part of a disaster."

"I'm not looking to end this. Just the opposite, in fact."

"You're in no place to want that."

Resigned to making his case once again, Kevin moved to his side next to her, propping his head on his upturned hand. "I feel terrible admitting this to myself, let alone anyone else, but the time I've spent with you has made me realize that my marriage was over a long time ago. I've become almost thankful to Deb for having an affair. I only wish it hadn't hurt my boys as much as it did."

"It hurt you, too."

"My pride more than my heart." He twirled a strand of her long blond hair around his finger. "If you take a chance on me—a real, all-in chance—I don't think it will be a disaster."

She was shaking her head before he finished speaking. "I don't do relationships, Kevin. I told you that from the beginning."

"I know you did, and I'm sure you have your reasons for that, but you've never told me what they are. If you're worried about me and where I am in all of this, I'm in."

"Isn't what we have good enough?"

"My twenty-year-old self would say hell yes, it's good enough. It's fucking fantastic. However, my fifty-year-old self wants more."

"My thirty-something self is in protection mode. I've seen this happen to my friends—they get involved with a guy fresh out of a long marriage, and after he sows some oats with them, he moves on to the one he wants to keep."

"I'm not looking to move on. If you think that, you haven't been paying attention." He slid his hand up her leg again, this time dragging her dress up to her waist, revealing the skimpy, sexy panties she favored. He'd become obsessed with her wide variety of skimpy panties.

"I have been paying attention, and I know you think you want more, but until you're actually divorced, we need to keep things the way they are now."

"I've filed, and it's in the works." He'd told her that, but it didn't hurt to remind her. "And you know I'm sticking around because I'm opening a practice here after the holidays." It wouldn't be as lucrative as his practice on the mainland had been, but it didn't need to be. He'd invested wisely and only needed to make enough to live comfortably.

"Let's revisit this when your divorce is final and see where we stand."

"I suppose that's fair enough." Rising to his knees, he helped her out of her dress and feasted his eyes on the sight of her creamy white skin and the scandalously sexy bra and panty set that she'd bought at Tiffany's shop. Among other things, he'd gotten her a five-hundred-dollar gift certificate to the shop for Christmas.

She sat up and started unbuttoning his shirt.

He reached behind her to release the hooks on her bra and watched her gorgeous breasts spring free of the tight confines of the bra. God, she was so sexy, and always so eager to have sex with him. He had to believe that underneath the insecurities she'd expressed about their current situation, she wanted the same things he did. So he would be patient. He would wait until he was actually divorced and then press her for a real commitment. They'd agreed to be monogamous while they were sleeping together, and that would have to be enough for now.

In the meantime, he'd talk to Dan Torrington tomorrow about speeding things up with Deb. His ex-wife had been blindsided when he filed for divorce, which led him to wonder if she'd been hoping for a reconciliation that wasn't going to happen.

He'd heard from his son Riley that her fling with the younger guy was over, so she might be having some regrets. That wasn't his problem. He'd meant what he said to Chelsea. Deb had done them both a favor by pulling the trigger to end a marriage that had withered on the vine a long time ago.

Chelsea wrapped her arms around him and peppered his chest with kisses, working her way down to his abdomen, which rippled under her soft lips.

Kevin knew where this was leading, and his cock got even harder from the anticipation. The heat of her mouth, the tight squeeze of her lips, the light suction and the swirl of her tongue got him every time. It had become a joke between them that he lost all control when she took him into her mouth, and this time was no exception.

"Baby, wait." Craving the closeness, he wanted to be inside her when he came. He withdrew from her mouth and brought her to the edge of the mattress before he removed her panties and feasted his eyes on her gorgeous body. Sexiest woman he'd ever been with, hands down. After worshiping her gorgeous breasts with his lips and tongue, he sank his fingers into her, gliding into her wet heat while pressing his thumb against her clit.

"Kevin," she gasped, arching into him, "*please.*"

After removing his fingers, he eased into her slowly, giving her time to adjust to and accommodate him before he picked up the pace, giving it to her hard and fast, the way she liked it best. They'd both gotten tested so they could forgo condoms, and what had already been exceptional before was now extraordinary. Since she'd already taken him to the edge with the spectacular blow job, he wouldn't last long. Wanting to make sure she was with him, he caressed her clit until he felt her clamp down on him as her body trembled with contractions. With her eyes closed, her lips parted and her breasts moving in time with his thrusts, she was like a goddess come to life, and he was determined to have her in his life forever.

Keeping that thought foremost in his mind, he slid his hands under her to clutch her ass as he came inside her, giving himself over to the incredible bliss he found in her arms every single time they were together.

CHAPTER 12

Slim Jackson left the McCarthys' party and headed out into the snow, jogging to the truck he kept on the island for days like this one when he couldn't use his motorcycle. He'd been on pins and needles all night, wanting to spend time with two people he admired greatly as well as their terrific family, but he was extremely eager to see Erin, too.

It'd been a long three months since he last saw her. While he worked in Florida during the off-season, they kept in touch through regular phone calls and FaceTime chats, getting to know each other better, which had been great. But it was no substitute for being with her in person.

He'd invited her to visit him in Florida, had gone so far as to offer to buy a plane ticket for her, but she'd declined for reasons she hadn't shared with him. Erin's refusal to visit had disappointed him more than he'd admitted to her. They'd formed a connection before he left that had only been strengthened by hours of conversation over the last few months. He couldn't understand why she didn't want to come visit him, and he hoped to get to the bottom of that while he was home for Christmas.

The road to the Southeast Light was long and dark, but Erin had left the gate open because he'd asked if he could stop by after the party. He had no idea what kind of reception to expect. The last time he saw her, the night Alex and Jenny got married, he'd brought her home after the wedding and kissed her good-night—a brief meeting of lips that had left him wanting so much more.

But he'd been expected in Miami the next day and hadn't had the time then to linger. He had time now, and he planned to linger—if she'd have him. As he approached the lighthouse, his heart began to beat faster, and a nervous flutter rippled through his stomach. When was the last time he'd been nervous to see a woman? High school?

Erin was different. He'd known that for a while now. She was special, and he wanted to get to know her even better, but she had walls on top of her walls, keeping him constantly striving to break them down and get to the heart of her. He wouldn't soon forget the night last summer when he'd shared with her that his given name was Tobias, the same name as her twin brother who'd been killed in the 9/11 attacks on New York City.

She'd been completely overwhelmed by that coincidence, and it had helped to bring them closer. But those damned walls kept getting in the way.

The glow of the light she'd left on over the back door lit his way from where he parked to the entrance to the lighthouse. He knocked on the door and then opened it to call up to her, banging the snow off his shoes on the welcome mat.

"Come on up," she said.

He took the spiral stairs two at a time, dying to see her gorgeous face and determine whether the things he'd felt for her last summer had grown in the months apart or morphed into something more like friendship than the romance he hoped for.

She waited for him at the top, wearing flannel pajama pants and a Gansett Island sweatshirt. Her chestnut-brown hair was in a high ponytail, her lovely face devoid of makeup. She took his breath away, especially when she stepped forward to welcome him with a long hug.

Slim wanted to keep her pressed up against him for as long as he possibly could, but they weren't "there" yet, so he released her reluctantly. At least one question had been answered to his satisfaction—this was still a potential romance and not just a really nice friendship.

"Hi, there," she said with a warm smile. Her brown eyes sparkled with delight as he removed his overcoat and hung it over the railing. "Wow, you look good."

He'd worn a navy blue suit with a white dress shirt and no tie to the party.

"And you're so tanned! You said you've been working nonstop in Florida."

"All work and no play makes Slim a dull boy."

She snickered. "That'll be the day. Who doesn't want your high-flying life?"

Who didn't, indeed? His lifestyle had suited him until lately, when he'd spent months living a thousand miles from a woman he couldn't stop thinking about.

"Drink?"

"I wouldn't say no to that." He hadn't touched a drop of alcohol at the party so he would be clearheaded when he saw her. But now that he was here, he could use a little liquid courage. Intrigued, he watched her make a Ketel One and soda on the rocks with a twist of lemon.

"Someone has been paying attention," he said when he took the drink from her with a grateful smile.

"I've watched you make that drink often enough on FaceTime."

"Not *that* often."

She raised a brow to challenge him and then further intrigued him when she made the same drink for herself. "I figured I ought to see what the hoopla was about."

He took a seat on her sofa, hoping she would join him—and sit close. Very close. "And?"

Much to his dismay, she sat on the other end of the sofa, facing him and curling her legs under her. "It's quite refreshing."

"I think so, too."

"I've never been much of a fan of vodka, but I have to say, it's pretty good."

"Vodka and I go *way* back." Winking at her, he added, "My mom couldn't smell it on my breath when I got home in high school."

"Ah-ha. I see how it was."

"I got in big trouble when I confessed that to her a few years ago."

Laughing, Erin said, "Why would you tell her that, ever?"

"She got me in a weak moment, and then informed me there's no statute of limitations on punishment for teenage crimes."

Still laughing, she said, "I think I'd like your mom."

"I know she'd like you." He swirled the ice around inside his glass and gave her a side-eyed glance. "You're kind of far away down there."

"Am I?"

"Uh-huh." He slid closer, leaving about a foot between them. Then he kicked off his dress shoes, put his feet on the coffee table and his head back against the sofa. "There. That's better."

"You look tired."

"Long day in the air."

"I wondered if you'd be able to get here with the snow."

"A little bit of snow wasn't going to ground me. Not when I had important business here today."

"How was the party?"

"It was great, but that wasn't my important business."

"No? What was?"

"As you well know, I couldn't wait to see you again. I've been counting the days."

"Have you?"

Nodding, he said, "Was I the only one counting?"

"No, you weren't. I was looking forward to today, too."

Encouraged by her honest reply, he gave her his most charming smile. He'd been told it could be rather potent. "Is that right?"

"I'd forgotten how handsome you are in a suit."

The unexpected compliment made his blood heat as it zinged through his veins. "And I'd forgotten how adorable you are in pajamas."

"You've never seen me in pajamas."

"Yes, I have. Remember the night I stayed with you after you hurt your ankle?"

"As I recall, I slept in my clothes."

"You did not. I helped you get changed, and believe me, I remember *every* detail."

"Why do *I* not remember that?"

"The pain muddled your brain."

"I think the vodka is muddling yours, and you're making stuff up."

He chuckled softly at her indignant reply. "Do you know one of the first things I noticed about you when Alex first introduced us is that you're a rare natural beauty? No enhancements needed."

"Oh, um, really?"

"Uh-huh. You know something else?"

"What?"

"I've spent the last few months asking myself over and over again why I didn't keep kissing you the night of his wedding." Leaning toward her, he said, "Why did I stop with just this?" He touched his lips to hers in imitation of the one fleeting kiss they'd shared in October. Like then, he immediately wanted more. But like then, the feeling that she was more fragile than she appeared kept him from taking what he wanted.

"You stopped again."

"So I did."

"How come?"

"I'm having a hard time getting a read on what you want."

"All those hours on the phone didn't tell you what I want?"

He took hold of her hand, aligning their palms and linking their fingers. "Not entirely."

"How long can you stay?"

"I'm here until after the New Year and then back to Florida through the end of March. Were you planning to go home to Pennsylvania for Christmas?"

"Well, I was until I heard this pilot friend of mine might be coming to town for the holidays."

"And what did your mom have to say about your change in plans?"

"To quote her directly, 'If I had a choice between here or there with that sexy pilot, I'd pick the pilot.'"

Slim tipped his head back and laughed. "I love your mom." He leaned in for another kiss, taking the time to linger now that he knew he was welcome to. "Twelve whole days together," he whispered. "I bet a lot can happen in that much time."

She curled her hand around his neck, drawing him into another kiss. "I can't wait to find out."

Snuggled up to her husband in comfy pajamas and her favorite robe with her children and grandchildren close by, a new ring on her finger and a glorious trip to look forward to, Linda decided this had been one of the very best days of her life. The time alone with Mac, the party and now this after-party in the salon of the Surf with Evan and Owen playing while the kids danced for them.

Hailey slept in her mother's arms. P.J. was out cold in Joe's arms, and Laura's son, Holden, snoozed on Owen's shoulder.

Betsy was curled up in Frank's lap with his arms around her while they chatted with Ned and Francine. Frankie had been so happy since he met Betsy, and Linda was thrilled for them both. Frank hadn't been seriously involved with anyone since he lost Jo, so it was particularly poignant to see him finding new love later in life.

Evan and Grace were beaming, back together after three long weeks apart. During the party, she'd noticed they were constantly touching each other and were obviously thrilled to be together again. She loved that and loved them together. She couldn't wait for their wedding in a few weeks.

Her mother radar had picked up something with Janey. She'd been quiet and withdrawn during the party and was listless now. Linda wondered if her daughter was coming down with something, which would be unfortunate timing for P.J.'s first Christmas. Tomorrow, she'd have a talk with her daughter to see what was going on.

Maddie hadn't confirmed her pregnancy, but after seeing her daughter-in-law pregnant twice before, Linda recognized the signs. She had a good feeling about this one. She remembered the terrible heartache of losing a baby followed by the cautious joy of learning they were expecting Mac. For nine long months, she'd practically held her breath waiting for something to go wrong until her son had arrived to make her a mother.

He'd been a joy to her every day of his life, never more so than in the years since he brought Maddie, Thomas and Hailey into their lives.

Linda's gaze landed on Abby, who was most definitely not herself. Something was wrong, but Abby and Adam had pretended otherwise for their sake tonight. The two of them were so in love that she couldn't imagine them having relationship issues. Tomorrow she would also see if she could find out what was troubling them.

She'd admit to having been skeptical of that pairing at first. After all, Abby had dated Grant for more than ten years, during which time there'd been no sign of the slightest spark between her and Adam—because there hadn't been one, according to both of them. She was grateful that both her sons had ended up with the women they loved and at no expense to their close relationship.

Speaking of Grant, he and his new wife, Stephanie, were so adorable together. She wondered if they were thinking of starting a family anytime soon. Grant wasn't getting any younger, so there was no time like the present, or so thought his future child's grandmother.

Her gaze shifted to Mallory. Though she was new to their family, sometimes it felt like she'd always been there. That was how seamlessly she'd fit in with her siblings and cousins. Linda hoped that she would spend more time with them after the New Year.

"You're quiet, my love," Mac said, rubbing her arm with his hand.

"Just taking it all in."

"It's a lot to take in."

"To think it began with you and me and led to this."

"It began with you and me forty years ago today."

She smiled at him and raised her glass to touch it to his. "You were right, you know."

He raised a rakish eyebrow. "About?"

"Everything. Us, the marina, the hotel, buying the house, raising the kids here. All of it. I don't know if I ever actually told you that. Everyone thought you were crazy for staking your claim here, but you knew exactly what you were doing."

"Hell, sweetheart," he said with a laugh, "I didn't know a damned thing other than I wanted you and I wanted Gansett. The rest was pure, dumb luck."

"It was a lot more than that, and you know it."

"None of it would've happened without you."

"Yes, it would have. You were on fire with ambition and determination."

"I was, but I wonder if I wouldn't have burned out here long before the marina took off if I hadn't had you to keep me company on all those cold winter nights."

"Cold winter nights are my favorite kind of nights," she said.

"Are you saying you're ready for bed?"

"Not quite yet, but soon."

"Say the word, and we're outta here."

"Before we do that…" When the boys were between songs, she cleared her throat to get everyone's attention. "Dad and I just want to say thank you all for a lovely celebration. We've had a wonderful forty years together, thanks mostly to our children and the ones they love. I couldn't have asked for a nicer day, and I just wanted to say thank you."

"It was all my idea," Mac said predictably, earning groans and sofa pillows thrown at him, all of which he dodged as he laughed.

"We have an announcement, too," Adam said, glancing at Abby, who seemed to grimace.

"Well, don't leave us hanging," Joe said.

"Abby and I are getting married on New Year's Eve, and you're all invited."

Linda hadn't seen that one coming, and why did the bride-to-be look less than thrilled by her fiancé's announcement? The room erupted into congratulations, and while she accepted everyone's good wishes, Abby looked like she was about to shatter.

What the heck was going on?

CHAPTER 13

"You shouldn't have told everyone until we're sure," Abby said an hour later when she and Adam were in their room upstairs.

"Until we were sure of what?" he asked as he unbuttoned his shirt.

She hated that baffled tone of his voice and hated that she'd given him reason to be baffled. She hated that both their lives had changed forever in that doctor's office yesterday. What had seemed so certain one day ago now was anything but.

"Until we're sure of what, Abby?"

"Our wedding. Everything."

"I'm sure, and you were too this morning when you said you'd marry me on New Year's Eve."

"I just... I... I can't seem to process any of it. The diagnosis, the wedding..." She shook her head in frustration and anguish.

Adam crossed the room to her, placing one hand on her shoulder and the other on her chin, compelling her to look at him. "You don't have to process any of it today or even tomorrow. We've got the rest of our lives to process anything that comes our way."

She couldn't bear to see the hurt and confusion in his beautiful blue eyes, so she looked away.

He gathered her in close to him. "Everything is going to be okay, Abs. If we stick together, we can get through this. I promise."

God, she wanted to lean on him. She wanted to hold on to him and never let go, but in the back of her mind was the nagging fear that it simply wasn't fair to shackle him to her when everything was so uncertain. He was saying and doing all the right things, and she appreciated his support so much, but that nagging doubt wouldn't be silenced.

"Let's get some sleep, honey. Tomorrow we'll make plans."

Abby let him lead her to bed, where she settled in her usual place—with her head on his shoulder, his arms around her. The thought of sleeping any other way but wrapped up in him was too painful to consider.

"I really loved the video," she said softly in the darkness, eager to think and talk about anything other than the elephant that sat squarely in the middle of the room. "You did such a great job."

"I'm glad you liked it." He ran a hand over her hair, trailing down to her back. "Someday we'll have our own video, packed with forty years of happy memories."

In the fog of her despair, Abby couldn't see that far into the future. She was having a hard time seeing next week or next month. She wanted to curl up in a ball and retreat from life, but Adam would never let her do that.

He turned to face her, keeping her head cushioned on his bicep. "I can hear your brain working a mile a minute."

"You cannot hear that."

"Yes, I can. I know you better than anyone else ever will, and I hear you thinking about all the ways this situation sucks and how unfair it is to me and all sorts of other things that would totally piss me off if you said them out loud."

Okay, so maybe he *could* hear her thoughts.

His lips found hers in the dark, and all the despair in the world couldn't keep her body from responding to him the way it always did. As his tongue slid between her lips to stroke hers, a sharp sting of desire between her legs had her squirming to get closer to him.

Under the T-shirt of his that she wore, his warm hand found her breast, rolling and teasing her nipple between his fingers as he continued to kiss her as if his life depended on reminding her of the fiery passion they shared.

Her T-shirt disappeared over her head. His shirt landed on the floor next to hers. When he brought his bare chest down on hers, Abby drew in a sharp breath at the glorious feeling of his skin rubbing against hers. That was one of her favorite things.

Adam broke the kiss and buried his face in the curve of her neck, making her shiver from the caress of his warm breath against her skin. "I love you more than anything else in this world, Abigail. If you leave me, you'll ruin my life and yours. Please don't leave me."

His softly spoken plea broke her heart. Adam, her Adam, didn't beg. He didn't plead. He didn't grovel. That she'd reduced him to all three was almost more than she could bear. Tears filled her eyes and slipped down the sides of her face, wetting her hair.

He kissed them away. And then his lips were closing around her nipple, making her moan from the pleasure that stripped away her worries. When Adam loved her, there was no space left in her mind for anything other than him and the exquisite way he made her feel. Her pajama pants and panties slid down her legs, which he pushed toward her chest as he bent to love her with his tongue.

Oh my God. "*Adam.*"

"Yeah, baby. I'm right here. I'll always be right here, and I'll always love you no matter what happens."

A sob hiccupped through her as he caressed her clit with his tongue and drove his fingers into her, sparking an orgasm that made her scalp tingle as she throbbed with aftershocks.

Giving her no time to recover and no chance to check out, he entered her slowly, grasping her ass in his big hands as he drove into her. She who had once had trouble taking a man into her body took this one like he was made for her, which he had been. She who'd had trouble having orgasms with other men had multiple orgasms with him, because he had accepted her completely and utterly, loving her exactly the way she was from the very beginning.

That thought finally broke her, and her deep sobs echoed through the small room.

Fully embedded in her, Adam wrapped his arms around her and held her as she cried. He had wanted her when she couldn't stand herself or her life and needed to shake things up. He'd wanted her after Cal rejected her. He'd wanted her when she had trouble reaching orgasm and when her body clenched up with nerves when they tried to have sex. He'd never given up on her, and he wouldn't give up now, either.

"Baby, talk to me. Tell me what you're thinking."

"I'm a f-fool," she said, hiccupping on the sobs.

When he started to withdraw from her, she stopped him with her hands on his ass, keeping him buried deep inside her.

"What do you mean?"

"You've always accepted me for who and what I am. That's why I fell in love with you."

He brushed the hair back from her face, and in the darkness, she could see the sparkle of his eyes as he gazed down at her. "I've never wanted you to be anything other than exactly who you are—flaws and all. Everyone has them, Abby. I'm not looking for perfect. I want you to come to me next week and marry me and take the plunge with me." As he spoke, he began to move in her again. "I want us to face down this health challenge together, and if necessary, adopt lots of babies to love and raise. We *will* have a family. I honestly don't care how it happens as long as you're the mom and I'm the dad."

Tears continued to leak from her eyes as his words washed over her like a balm, soothing the open wound inside her.

"We'll find you the best doctors in the country, and we'll keep you healthy no matter what we have to do. I need you with me for the rest of my life. You have no idea how much I love you. No idea at all."

Except she did know. He'd shown her every day for more than a year now, and he'd never wavered in his acceptance of her. That was the one thing that had been lacking in her other relationships. She'd never felt truly accepted. Until Adam had rescued her from herself last summer and shown her what it meant to be truly and completely loved.

"I'm sorry," she whispered.

"For what?"

"For thinking that you'd be better off without me."

"Don't ever think that. When I say you'd ruin me if you left me, I'm not kidding."

She ran her fingers through his thick, dark hair and kissed him. "I know."

"Tell me you love me, too. Tell me you believe me when I say I'll stand by you no matter how bad it gets. I need to know—"

"I love you, Adam, and I believe you."

"Tell me you also believe that I'd rather have you and any challenges you may face because of your diagnosis than a perfectly healthy woman who isn't you."

"I do. I believe that."

His lips curved into a smile on top of hers. "Let me hear that first part again."

"Which part?"

"The 'I do' part."

Abby returned his smile. "I do, Adam. I choose you to be mine, and I believe you when you tell me how much you love me."

He turned his face away and blew out a deep breath that sounded an awful lot like relief to her. "Thank God for that. You've had me freaking out all day about what I'd do if you tried to run away from me."

"You wouldn't let me get away."

"No, I wouldn't."

She raised her hips to remind him of what they'd been doing before her emotional meltdown.

With his arms tight around her and his lips devouring hers, he rocked into her, thrusting deep the way she liked it best, until she broke the kiss to cry out from the pleasure that shot through her body.

Adam groaned and got impossibly harder and bigger inside her before he came, his fingers digging into her shoulders.

"Love you forever, Abby."

"Love you forever, Adam."

"So, New Year's Eve? Yes?"

"I can't wait."

CHAPTER 14

New Year's Eve on Gansett Island dawned sunny and cold, the perfect sort of day for a winter wedding. Linda carried mugs of coffee upstairs for her and Mac to enjoy in bed. With nowhere to be until later, they had time for a lazy morning.

Adam is getting married, she thought with a sigh. He was her baby who wasn't a baby anymore and hadn't been for a very long time. No matter. He would always be *her* baby.

"What're you sighing about, my love?" Mac asked when she handed him one of the mugs. He was propped up in bed, reading the morning headlines on the iPad the kids had given him for Christmas. With glasses propped on the end of his nose and his hair tousled from sleep, he looked sexy and adorable.

She slid into bed next to him, careful not to spill the coffee on the crisp white sheets. "*Adam* is getting *married*."

"So I've heard. This is a good thing, no?"

"Of course it is, but I'm still allowed to feel a little melancholy about another of my babies taking the plunge."

"Should I not mention that Evan will take the plunge in exactly nineteen days?"

Linda moaned. "No, you shouldn't."

He chuckled at her foolishness. "I love that they've each found their perfect match."

"So do I. Don't get me wrong. It's just…"

"They grew up way too fast."

"Yes. That."

"I know, babe. I think about that all the time. Seems like five minutes ago, we had a house full of screaming rug rats, and now…"

"Silence."

"And while silence can be golden, it happened fast."

"We haven't had much of a chance to talk about what Adam told us last night."

"I've been reading up about this condition Abby has." He turned the iPad so she could see. "It's difficult but manageable from all accounts. Fertility can be a big challenge."

"I hate that for them. They'd have such beautiful babies."

"Yes, they would, and it's very possible they will. It'll just take some doing."

"If anyone can get through this, it's those two. They're so perfect for each other. It's funny how I never would've thought so back when she was dating Grant, but now…"

"You can't picture her with anyone but Adam and vice versa."

"Right."

He put his iPad and mug on the bedside table and turned to her. "Speaking of babies, what do we think about Janey being pregnant again?"

"We think it's very scary."

"I gotta be honest—as much as I want another grandbaby, I sort of wish they'd quit with P.J."

"They planned to, but you know what happens when people make plans."

Mac reached for her hand. "Joe said they're going to the mainland early and she'll be admitted for the last few weeks so there's no chance of what happened last time happening again."

"There's always a chance, but at least she'll be already in the hospital if it does. Then there's Maddie."

"What about her?"

"She's pregnant again, even if they're not saying so yet."

"How do you know that?"

She gave him her best withering look. "Hello? Because I know everything."

"You're getting a little full of yourself over there," he said with a teasing smile.

"You mark my words. She's pregnant, or my name isn't Voodoo Mama."

"What do you think of Evan and Grace's plan to ride the music wave?" he asked. It had been a rather eventful holiday season for the McCarthy family.

"As much as I want them here with us, I think they're doing the right thing. He would've always wondered what might've been if he didn't seize this moment."

"I agree. It's not every day an artist has a song go to number one. He would wonder, and she would feel like she kept him from chasing his dream. That they found a way to chase it together is fantastic. I love that she found someone to manage the pharmacy for her and Josh agreed to take on the studio while Evan is on the road."

"It all worked out perfectly. I also hear that Stephanie decided to go to LA with Grant after all."

"Oh, that's good news. I wasn't happy about the idea of them spending all that time apart when they're newlyweds."

"Me either, but we couldn't blame her about being hesitant to relive the nightmare of Charlie's incarceration."

"No, definitely not."

"So five children happily married or soon to be. That leaves Mallory."

"I've been thinking a lot about her since she went back to Providence," Mac said. "She doesn't say much about her past or her love life, but I get the feeling she hasn't had it easy when it comes to men."

"She said she's not married 'anymore,' but that's all she's said to me."

"Me too. I'm dying to know more, but I don't want to push her to confide in me until she's ready to."

"That's a wise approach. Baby steps, my darling."

"That's not really my style," he said with a sheepish grin.

"No, really?" she asked, laughing. "This is no time for your bull-in-a-china-shop approach to fatherhood, Mac."

"That's not nice."

"Is it untrue?"

"It's not *completely* untrue."

Chuckling, Linda said, "What time does she get in today for the wedding?"

"She worked last night, so she's on the four o'clock boat. I'm picking her up."

"We'll have this weekend with her and then the week in Anguilla for Grace and Evan's wedding." Thankfully, they'd managed to relocated their wedding to another resort when the original one had been closed down for repairs after a storm. "You'll have a chance to get to know her even better without overwhelming her."

"Yes, dear." He kissed the back of her hand. "What do you feel like doing today?"

"As little as possible. I'm still recovering from the madness that is Christmas around here."

"Another spectacular job from Linda McCarthy holiday productions."

"I'm glad you thought so. Thank God Maddie did Christmas Eve and that everyone pitches in to help on Christmas Day. All that help makes it easier on Mom than it used to be when everything fell to me."

"You make it look easy."

"Weren't the kids so cute?"

"*So* cute. I forgot how fun it is to have little ones underfoot on Christmas. You want to see the pictures again?"

"I sure do."

They spent the rest of the morning scrolling through the hundreds of photos he'd taken with his new toy during the holidays—and they watched the video Adam had made for their anniversary for about the hundredth time. It never got old, and every time she watched it, Linda saw something she hadn't noticed before.

Adam was getting *married…*

As her eyes filled with tears, she hoped that by the time six o'clock rolled around, she'd be ready to once again be mother of the groom.

*

Adam and Abby had overtaken the McCarthy's Gansett Island Inn for their wedding. Copying Laura's idea, they'd arranged for rooms for everyone at the inn so family members could party the night away without having to drive home afterward. The inn was still beautifully decorated for the holidays, and everything was in place for the wedding.

Daisy Babson, head of housekeeping, had stepped up to help finalize their plans since the hotel's event coordinator was on vacation. They couldn't have pulled off the wedding on such short notice without Daisy's able assistance.

"To say event planning isn't your specialty, you sure arranged a miracle," Adam said he and Abby walked with Daisy through the downstairs rooms that would be used for the wedding.

"I'm so glad you're happy with it." Daisy glowed with happiness after getting a big engagement ring from Dr. David Lawrence for Christmas. "It's been good practice for planning my own wedding."

"We're all so happy for you guys," Adam said.

"Thank you. I know it means a lot to David to have your family's support."

It seemed like a long time now since David's relationship with Janey had ended with him cheating on her. David had changed a lot in the last few years and had earned the McCarthy family's undying respect when he delivered both Hailey and P.J. under difficult—and dangerous—conditions.

"How did he ask you?" Abby asked.

"It was very romantic and sweet," Daisy said, blushing lightly as she conveyed the details of the proposal. "After we spent Christmas Day with his family, we came home to our place. He said he had one more gift he'd forgotten to give me earlier. I almost passed out when I realized what was happening."

Abby laughed at the comical expression on Daisy's face.

"It was perfect," Daisy declared.

Abby hugged her. "I'm so happy for you. No one deserves to be swept off her feet more than you do."

Adam wanted to tell his bride that she deserved it, too, but rather than tell her, he intended to show her. Later.

He and Abby had said to hell with superstition and had spent their wedding day together. In truth, he was still slightly afraid to let her out of his sight. Since their intense conversation on the night of his parents' anniversary party, she'd been more resigned to her diagnosis. She'd been an enthusiastic if quieter-than-usual participant in the planning of their wedding. However, he still sensed an underlying fragility to her newfound strength, which was why they'd spent every day this week together.

He'd taken the week off from work and had given her his undivided attention. With her store closed down for the winter as of Christmas Eve, they focused on resting and relaxing in the days before their wedding. Adam couldn't wait to give her the surprise he had for her later.

She'd suggested that the week in Anguilla for Evan's wedding could count as their honeymoon, but Adam didn't want to wait three weeks to celebrate their marriage. They were leaving tomorrow for a weeklong cruise to the Bahamas, and he was excited to have his new wife completely to himself for a whole week.

Hell, he was excited about everything where she was concerned—the good, the bad, the sickness, the health and everything in between. After his last relationship ended in spectacular fashion, he'd been resigned to spending the rest of his life alone rather than ending up with the wrong person.

At the lowest moment in his life, he'd come home to Gansett and found true love with his brother's ex-girlfriend. He hadn't seen it coming, but that was what made it so great. They'd been right under each other's noses for years without realizing they were destined to be together.

As Abby chatted with Daisy about the flower delivery that would arrive from the florist, Adam squeezed her hand.

She replied with the genuine smile he hadn't seen much of since her diagnosis, but it gave him hope that she would bounce back in due time. That she also looked excited about the wedding helped to soothe his battered nerves.

The rest of the day flew by with last-minute details and other preparations. With darkness descending as it did so early in the winter, Adam spent his last few minutes as a single man in the hotel salon with his brothers as well as Joe and Owen, all of whom were serving as his groomsmen. His nephew, Thomas, was the ring bearer. Owen was doing double duty and would provide music for the ceremony. Adam's Uncle Frank would preside.

Abby had asked Grace to be her maid of honor with Janey, Maddie, Laura and Stephanie as her attendants. They hadn't had time to come up with the usual matching outfits, so all the girls were wearing black cocktail dresses, and the guys were in dark suits. Abby had found a dress she loved at Tiffany's store a couple of months ago, and Adam couldn't wait to see it.

It had been rather easy to throw together an elegant last-minute wedding that would also serve as a New Year's Eve party.

"Are you ready, bro?" Mac asked, clasping Adam's shoulder.

"So ready."

His brother Grant shook his hand. "Take good care of Abby. She deserves the very best."

"She'll never get anything less than that from me."

Grant nodded soberly. Adam was thankful that there'd never been any ill will from his brother when he started seeing Abby. Grant knew he'd screwed up with her, and he'd told Adam that his experience with Abby had prepared him to do better with Stephanie. Everyone had ended up where they belonged, but it was still a relief not to have trouble with Grant. That would've forced Adam to make some awful decisions.

Evan approached him with a white rose, a huge pin and a demonic look in his eyes.

"Don't even think about it, idiot."

"I only thought about it. I wasn't actually going to do it." Evan, the best man, pinned the rose onto Adam's lapel and then took a measuring perusal of Adam's appearance. "You won't ruin the pictures."

Adam laughed. He expected nothing less from Evan. The two of them had spent their childhood beating the crap out of each other every chance they got, and were still known to wrestle on occasion. In fact, they'd gotten in trouble for wrestling too close to their mother's tree on Christmas Day. Good times.

Despite the fighting—or maybe because of it—he and Evan were close, and there was no one else he'd rather have stand up for him today. He hoped Evan would resist the urge to headlock him during the ceremony.

Adam checked his watch. Ten minutes until six. Ten minutes until he married the love of his life. He couldn't wait.

*

Clutching the arm of her father and following her attendants, Abby made her way downstairs to the salon, where she and Adam would exchange vows. The beautiful old hotel was awash in candlelight that created a soft, romantic vibe. She'd been skeptical that they could pull off a decent wedding with only eleven days to prepare, but as usual, Adam had shown her that anything was possible if you wanted it badly enough.

With every step she took toward her groom, Abby thought about the long journey she had traveled to arrive at this moment. More than ten years with Grant had led to heartache in the end, followed by another failed relationship with Cal—and a broken engagement.

She'd officially given up on men and love, which was exactly when her path had collided with Adam's on a ferry ride home to Gansett that changed both their lives forever.

Even though her relationship with Adam was totally different from anything she'd known before, she'd still expected something to go wrong—because in her experience, something always went wrong. The devastating diagnosis last week had nearly derailed them, but he hadn't let it. He hadn't let her withdraw into herself. He'd fought for her and for them the way he always had and, she now knew, the way he always would.

She'd chosen an off-white silk dress with a deep V neckline that showed off the cleavage Adam loved. It fell to her ankles and included a slit on the right side. The dress was sexier than she'd normally have chosen for herself, but if her body was going to change dramatically due to her disorder, she wanted Adam to have the memory of a sexy, beautiful bride to cherish.

Abby had left her hair down because that was how he liked it best, and had worn the lightest possible amount of makeup. Marrying him was a dream come true, and she didn't want to be unrecognizable to him. She and her dad turned the last corner before they entered the room where the ceremony would be held, and Abby took a deep breath, preparing herself for him.

She squeezed her dad's arm, and they rounded the corner. Accompanied by the gentle tone of Owen's guitar, Abby locked eyes with Adam, who appeared to brush a tear from his cheek. He was so beautiful and so sexy and all hers forever. In those final steps as a single woman, she let go of her painful past and her worries about the future. For right now, there was only Adam and her and the vows they would make to each other.

Adam shook hands with her dad and tucked her hand into the crook of his elbow, squeezing it once in reassurance. "Stunning," he whispered.

"Likewise," she replied, smiling up at him.

"We've come together tonight to celebrate the marriage of my wonderful nephew Adam with his beautiful Abby." Frank led them through the traditional recitation of vows and the exchange of rings that they'd ordered online and paid top dollar to have shipped to them in time for the wedding. "In addition to the vows they've already taken, Adam and Abby have written their own vows. Adam?"

As he took a deep breath, his eyes shone with unshed tears. "My whole life began the day I found you on that ferry ride home to Gansett," he said gruffly, bringing tears to her eyes, too. "We were both at the lowest point in our lives and in no way prepared for what was about to happen to us. Since that momentous day, you have taken me places I never expected to go, including the tattoo parlor."

Abby laughed, as did everyone else.

Adam touched his lips to the new tattoo of their wedding date on her inner wrist. He had the same one in the same place.

Releasing one of her hands, he cupped her face as he gazed into her eyes. "No matter what challenges may come our way, I've always got your back, and I know you've got mine, too. I love every single thing about you, and I always will."

He used his thumbs to brush away her tears.

"I have never been more myself than I am with you," Abby said. "I've never felt as completely accepted as I am with you. And I'll never love anyone the way I love you. From those first moments on the ferry, you've taken care of me and protected me and encouraged me to go for what I want, even if it might seem out of reach. You've shown me that nothing is out of reach when you have the right person holding your hand through life's challenges. The day I found you on the ferry was the best day of my life, until today."

Before Frank could tell him it was time, Adam kissed her, and Frank declared them husband and wife.

"I'd tell you to kiss your bride, Adam," Frank said, "but you've got that covered."

Adam kissed her for a long time—so long that Abby began to burn with embarrassment as their family and friends laughed. She was about to break the kiss when he withdrew slowly, smiling brightly at her.

"Ladies and gentlemen," Frank said, "I present to you Adam and Abby McCarthy."

As their guests cheered, Adam raised their joined hands to his lips and kissed the back of hers.

Finally, Abby thought. Finally, she'd gotten her happily ever after, and the best part was she got to spend the rest of her life with him.

EPILOGUE

"Four down, two to go," Big Mac said to Linda as the clock headed for midnight and the party raged on around them. Jackets and heels had come off, ties were strewn over backs of chairs, and the champagne continued to flow.

The bride and groom were right in the middle of it all, dancing with their siblings and friends and having a generally fantastic time from what he could see. Tonight there had been no sign of the troubling diagnosis that had thrown them for a loop. Tonight had been all about celebration.

"It was a beautiful wedding," Linda said.

"They're a beautiful couple."

"Look at them all. They're incredible. Every single one of them—the ones we gave birth to and the ones we've picked up along the way."

"They certainly are." He took advantage of the opportunity to kiss her. "I can't wait to see what the next forty years brings."

"Neither can I."

With his arms around her, Big Mac drew her into his embrace, looking forward to everything still to come with his own bride.

***

I hope you enjoyed *Celebration After Dark* and the look back at how Mac and Linda came to be. If you wondered where the McCarthy boys came by their formidable charm, you probably aren't wondering anymore. I loved writing Mac and Linda's story and looking back to before the marina and the hotel were successful businesses. Everyone starts somewhere, and they were no different. To chat about the story with spoilers allowed, join the Celebration After Dark Reader Group at www.facebook.com/groups/CelebrationAfterDark/. If you're not one of the nearly 10,000 members of the McCarthy Series Reader Group, get on over to our online Tiki Bar and join the fun at www.facebook.com/groups/McCarthySeries/.

The Gansett Island Series continues in 2016 with *Desire After Dark*, Slim and Erin's story. Watch for more information coming soon! To be kept informed of new books, make sure you're on my email newsletter list. You can join at marieforce.com on the left-hand side, where it asks for your name and email address. This is the best way to ensure you never miss a new book, a giveaway or a possible appearance in your area.

Thanks as always to my amazing team: Julie Cupp, CMP, Lisa Cafferty, CPA, Holly Sullivan, Isabel Sullivan, Nikki Colquhoun, Cheryl Serra, Ashley Lopez and Courtney Lopes. Linda Ingmanson, copy editor on all my self-published books—thank you so much for always squeezing me in when I need you. Thank you Anne Woodall, Kara Conrad and Ronlyn Howe for being my beta readers, and to Holly, who is always my FIRST reader. Thank you, Holly!

To the Gansett Island faithful who make it SO FUN to continue writing this series after seven years, you have my eternal gratitude. I never thought I'd be saying the words *Book 15 with no end in sight*. This series has made my career, and that couldn't have happened without all of you.

xoxo

Marie

Coming in 2016! *Desire After Dark*, **Slim and Erin's story!**

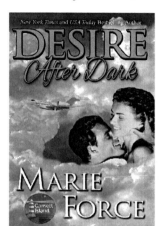

Tobias "Slim" Jackson has the perfect life as a pilot on Gansett Island in the summer and in Florida in the winter. He's happiest when he's in the air, or at least that was the case before last summer when he met Erin Barton, Gansett Island's newest lighthouse keeper. Now he can't seem to find his usual enthusiasm for flying, winter in the sunny South or anything that doesn't include her.

Erin has been stuck on pause since she lost her twin brother. She'll tell you herself that her life has been a hot mess since Toby died. After dropping out of law school, she's flitted from one pointless job to another, existing rather than truly living. Then she comes to Gansett Island to take over as the new lighthouse keeper and meets Slim, who happens to share her beloved brother's first name. That small coincidence is enough to convince Erin that she needs to spend more time with the dashing pilot—except for the fact that he's spending the winter more than a thousand miles from her.

Now Slim's come home to Gansett for the holidays and to hopefully pick up where he left off with Erin. He's got twelve days before he's due back in Florida to finish out the remainder of his winter obligations. A lot can happen in twelve days, but will it be enough to convince Erin that it's time to start truly living again? Read

Slim and Erin's story and catch up with the rest of the Gansett Island cast in *Desire After Dark*, coming in 2016! Join my mailing list at marieforce.com to be notified when the preorder is available.

OTHER TITLES BY MARIE FORCE

Love Always Boxed Set, First Books in Four of Marie's Bestselling Series

Contemporary Romances Available from Marie Force
The Gansett Island Series

Gansett Island Boxed Set, Books 1-3 (ebook only)

Gansett Island Boxed Set, Books 4-6 (ebook only)

Gansett Island Boxed Set, Books 7-9 (ebook only)

Book 1: Maid for Love

Book 2: Fool for Love

Book 3: Ready for Love

Book 4: Falling for Love

Book 5: Hoping for Love

Book 6: Season for Love

Book 7: Longing for Love

Book 8: Waiting for Love

Book 9: Time for Love

Book 10: Meant for Love

Book 10.5: Chance for Love, *A Gansett Island Novella*

Book 11: Gansett After Dark

Book 12: Kisses After Dark

Book 13: Love After Dark

Book 14: Celebration After Dark

The Treading Water Series

10th Anniversary Treading Water Boxed Set (ebook)

Book 1: Treading Water

Book 2: Marking Time

Book 3: Starting Over

Book 4: Coming Home

The Green Mountain Series

Book 1: All You Need Is Love

Book 2: I Want to Hold Your Hand

Book 3: I Saw Her Standing There

Book 4: And I Love Her

Novella: You'll Be Mine

Book 5: It's Only Love

Book 6: Ain't She Sweet

Single Titles

The Single Titles Boxed Set

Georgia on My Mind

True North

The Fall

Everyone Loves a Hero

Love at First Flight

Line of Scrimmage

Books from M. S. Force
The Erotic Quantum Series
Book 1: Virtuous

Book 2: Valorous

Book 3: Victorious

Book 4: Rapturous

Romantic Suspense Novels Available from Marie Force
The Fatal Series
One Night With You, A Fatal Series Prequel Novella

Book 1: Fatal Affair

Book 2: Fatal Justice

Book 3: Fatal Consequences

Book 3.5: Fatal Destiny, The Wedding Novella

Book 4: Fatal Flaw

Book 5: Fatal Deception

Book 6: Fatal Mistake

Book 7: Fatal Jeopardy

Book 8: Fatal Scandal

Book 9: Fatal Frenzy

Single Title
The Wreck

ABOUT THE AUTHOR

Marie Force is the *New York Times* bestselling author of contemporary romance, including the Gansett Island Series, which has sold more than 2.2 million books, and the Fatal Series from Harlequin Books, which has sold more than 1 million books. In addition, she is the author of the Green Mountain Series from Berkley Publishing as well as the new erotic romance Quantum Series, written under the slightly modified name of M.S. Force.

Her goals in life are simple—to finish raising two happy, healthy, productive young adults, to keep writing books for as long as she possibly can and to never be on a flight that makes the news.

Join Marie's mailing list for news about new books and upcoming appearances in your area. Follow her on Twitter @marieforce and on Facebook. Join one of Marie's many reader groups. Contact Marie at *marie@marieforce.com*. Subscribe to my new blog to hear the latest and greatest news, including giveaways and other great prizes. Go to the blog website and enter your email address on the upper right-hand side.

CPSIA information can be obtained at www.ICGtesting.com
Printed in the USA
LVOW07s0522271115

464318LV00015B/811/P